You're About to Become a
Privileged Woman.

INTRODUCING
PAGES & PRIVILEGES™.

It's our way of thanking you for buying
our books at your favorite retail store.

— *GET ALL THIS FREE* —
WITH JUST ONE PROOF OF PURCHASE:

◆ Hotel Discounts up to 60% at home and abroad

◆ Travel Service - Guaranteed lowest published
  airfares plus 5% cash back on tickets

◆ $25 Travel Voucher

◆ Sensuous Petite Parfumerie collection ($50 value)

◆ Insider Tips Letter with sneak previews of
  upcoming books

◆ Mystery Gift (if you enroll before 6/15/95)

You'll get a FREE personal card, too.
It's your passport to all these benefits— and to
even more great gifts & benefits to come!

There's no club to join. No purchase commitment. No obligation.

As a *Privileged Woman*, you'll be entitled to all these *Free Benefits*. And *Free Gifts*, too.

To thank you for buying our books, we've designed an exclusive FREE program called *PAGES & PRIVILEGES™*. You can enroll with just one Proof of Purchase, and get the kind of luxuries that, until now, you could only read about.

*B*IG HOTEL DISCOUNTS

A privileged woman stays in the finest hotels. And so can you—at up to 60% off! Imagine standing in a hotel check-in line and watching as the guest in front of you pays $150 for the same room that's only costing you $60. Your *Pages & Privileges* discounts are good at Sheraton, Marriott, Best Western, Hyatt and thousands of other fine hotels all over the U.S., Canada and Europe.

*F*REE DISCOUNT TRAVEL SERVICE

A privileged woman is always jetting to romantic places. When <u>you</u> fly, just make one phone call for the lowest published airfare at time of booking—<u>or double the difference back</u>! PLUS—

you'll get a $25 voucher to use the first time you book a flight AND <u>5% cash back on every ticket you buy thereafter through the travel service</u>!

FREE GIFTS!

A privileged woman is always getting wonderful gifts.
Luxuriate in rich fragrances that will stir your senses (and his). This gift-boxed assortment of fine perfumes includes three popular scents, each in a beautiful designer bottle. <u>Truly Lace</u>...This luxurious fragrance unveils your sensuous side. <u>L'Effleur</u>...discover the romance of the Victorian era with this soft floral. <u>Muguet des bois</u>...a single note floral of singular beauty. This $50 value is yours—FREE when you enroll in *Pages & Privileges*! And it's just the beginning of the gifts and benefits that will be coming your way!

FREE INSIDER TIPS LETTER

A privileged woman is always informed. And you'll be, too, with our free letter full of fascinating information and sneak previews of upcoming books.

MORE GREAT GIFTS & BENEFITS TO COME

A privileged woman always has a lot to look forward to.
And so will you. You get all these wonderful FREE gifts and benefits now with only one purchase...and there are no additional purchases required. However, each additional retail purchase of Harlequin and Silhouette books brings you a step closer to even more great FREE benefits like half-price movie tickets...and even more FREE gifts like these beautiful fragrance gift baskets:

L'Effleur ...This basketful of romance lets you discover L'Effleur from head to toe, heart to home.

Truly Lace ...A basket spun with the sensuous luxuries of Truly Lace, including Dusting Powder in a reusable satin and lace covered box.

ENROLL NOW!
Complete the Enrollment Form on the back of this card and become a Privileged Woman today!

Enroll Today in *PAGES & PRIVILEGES*™, the program that gives you Great Gifts and Benefits with just one purchase!

Enrollment Form

☐ *Yes!* I WANT TO BE A *Privileged Woman.*

Enclosed is one *PAGES & PRIVILEGES*™ Proof of Purchase from any Harlequin or Silhouette book currently for sale in stores (Proofs of Purchase are found on the back pages of books) and the store cash register receipt. Please enroll me in *PAGES & PRIVILEGES*™. Send my Welcome Kit and FREE Gifts -- and activate my FREE benefits -- immediately.

NAME (please print)

ADDRESS   APT. NO

CITY   STATE   ZIP/POSTAL CODE

NO CLUB!
NO COMMITMENT!
Just one purchase brings you great Free Gifts and Benefits!
(See inside for details.)

Please allow 6-8 weeks for delivery. Quantities are limited. We reserve the right to substitute items. Enroll before October 31, 1995 and receive one full year of benefits.

▶ DETACH HERE AND MAIL TODAY! ▶

Name of store where this book was purchased_____

Date of purchase_____

Type of store:

☐ Bookstore   ☐ Supermarket   ☐ Drugstore

☐ Dept. or discount store (e.g. K-Mart or Walmart)

☐ Other (specify)_____

Which Harlequin or Silhouette series do you usually read?

_____

Complete and mail with one Proof of Purchase and store receipt to:

U.S.: *PAGES & PRIVILEGES*™, P.O. Box 1960, Danbury, CT 06813-1960

Canada: *PAGES & PRIVILEGES*™, 49-6A The Donway West, P.O. 813, North York, ON M3C 2E8   PRINTED IN U.S.A

"*I am* not *promiscuous!*"

"Good," Benedict replied, adding dangerously, "because I'm not paying my caretaker to have sex!"

"How dare you!" Vanessa hissed furiously, outraged by his crudity.

"Prim and proper won't wash anymore, Flynn. I dare because I pay the bills here, and therefore I get to set the rules of conduct." He gave her a narrow-eyed look. "Just remember—under my roof, you're as celibate as a nun!"

SUSAN NAPIER was born on St. Valentine's Day, so it's not surprising she has developed an enduring love of romantic stories. She started her writing career as a journalist in Auckland, New Zealand, trying her hand at romance fiction only after she had married her handsome boss! Numerous books later, she still lives with her most enduring hero, and two future heroes—her sons!—two cats and a computer. When she's not writing, she likes to read and cook, often simultaneously!

Books by Susan Napier

HARLEQUIN PRESENTS
1595—WINTER OF DREAMS
1674—THE CRUELLEST LIE
1707—PHANTOM LOVER

Savage Courtship

Harlequin Books

TORONTO • NEW YORK • LONDON
AMSTERDAM • PARIS • SYDNEY • HAMBURG
STOCKHOLM • ATHENS • TOKYO • MILAN
MADRID • WARSAW • BUDAPEST • AUCKLAND

ISBN 0-373-11744-2

SAVAGE COURTSHIP

Copyright © 1994 by Susan Napier.

First North American Publication 1995.

Printed in U.S.A.

CHAPTER ONE

IT WAS dark inside the big stone house but the lack of light didn't hamper the man gliding silently up the narrow stairway. He moved with the sure-footed ease of someone used to exploiting the full potential of his subsidiary senses. He hadn't needed to be able to see to quietly open the locked front door, double-shrouded in the night-shadow of the portico, and once inside he had found the stairs by instinctively measuring his stride, shifting his double burden to his right hand so that he could plot his upward progress on the smooth banister-rail with his left.

At the top of the stairs he strode confidently into the inky blackness, mentally centring himself between the pale walls to avoid the occasional dark lump of furniture that jutted out into the narrow passageway. Several metres down he turned abruptly to his left, reaching down for a low door-handle and entering the room beyond without even breaking his stride.

When he closed the door behind him the darkness was almost complete and after the briefest of hesitations he walked over to the far wall where he grasped a handful of thick fabric and dragged it aside, revealing a row of narrow windows that overlooked a small, starlit black lake. The smooth yet shifting reflective surface was oddly disorientating, the familiar beacon of the Southern Cross glinted up at him from below, as well as tracing its unique pattern of stars across the midnight vault of heaven.

His hand slowly fisted and then relaxed against the window-frame and, as if the simple action had pumped all the tension out of his body, he slumped, uttering a long sigh of relief as he set the hard, slim case and its soft-sided companion carefully on the floor beside him. He leaned against the windowsill for long moments, an obscure silhouette of dark on dark, his forehead resting against the cool glass. Then, with another sigh, he shrugged himself upright again, rolling his head around on his shoulders in the universal gesture of exhaustion, rubbing his neck with his hand as his soft-soled black shoes padded across the polished wood floor towards a second, shadowy door.

Benedict Savage narrowed his eyes to protect himself against the initial dazzling burst of light in the small bathroom as he flicked on the switch by the door and then leaned over and spun the shower tap to the pre-set pressure and temperature he preferred—strong and almost unbearably hot. He took off his tortoiseshell-framed spectacles and tossed them carelessly on to the marble vanity unit as he rubbed the narrow bridge of his nose.

He couldn't remember ever having felt this bone-weary before—perhaps because usually any tiredness on the return trip to New Zealand was masked by the sense of euphoria generated by the completion of yet another commission. This time the euphoria had been riddled with an indefinable dissatisfaction that had infuriated him, since the work he had produced had been arguably the best of his success-studded career. Perhaps he had just worked too hard for too long on this one—had wanted it too much. There was bound to be a feeling of anticlimax, especially since he had nothing half as exciting lined up to tackle next.

Benedict shook his head to try and clear the miasma of exhaustion that thickened his thoughts.

He stripped off his tailored suit and ultra-conservative shirt and tie, tossing the separate pieces carelessly across the willow-cane hamper in the corner, a grim smile touching his thin mouth as he contemplated the possibility that age was starting to catch up with him. Tomorrow was his thirty-fourth birthday and, although he was confident that he was still at the peak of his intellectual abilities, perhaps his body was telling him it was time to ease up on a relentless regime of travel-work-travel.

This particular flight across the world had been a nightmare of foul-ups and delays, and he had come perilously close to losing his famed cool. That more than anything told him that it might be time for a serious assessment of his priorities.

Benedict stepped into the shower, glancing briefly at his reflection in the steamy mirror as he pulled the glass door closed, noting with a clinical satisfaction that he didn't look as wretchedly jaded as he felt. The eyes that felt gritty and bloodshot were their usual cool, clear blue and he had the kind of olive complexion that didn't readily show the lines of tension that he could feel pulling tightly beneath his skin. His short-cropped black hair might be streaked with premature grey, but his body was as lean and hard as it ever had been, thanks partly to genetics but mostly to his habit of never taking up residence in a hotel or apartment block that didn't have a swimming-pool. His days always started with a mile of laps, the solitary rhythm soothing his mind as it sharpened his muscles.

The hot shower did its job, loosening his aching joints and easing the tightness in skin desiccated by aircraft air-conditioning. His thoughts drifted on a pleasant plateau of mindless fatigue. He stepped out of the shower cubicle and blotted himself roughly with the thick white towel from the heated towel-rail, too sluggish to notice its faint dampness. Dropping it lazily underfoot, he flicked off the light and padded back into the bedroom, rubbing his strong fingers across his sandpaper jaw, grateful that there was no reason to have to shave again before falling into bed. More than one woman had commented on the intriguing contrast between a beard that grew so quickly and his hairless chest.

He snapped on the standard lamp by the window and opened the casements, enjoying the warm flow of fresh air over his damp skin. Auckland in late March could be chilly, but tonight the region was still palpably in the grip of sultry summer. He stretched, slow and hard, prolonging a shuddering yawn as he savoured a pleasurable sense of anticipation. He removed his steel Rolex and dropped it on to the pristine white blotter on the desk which also served as a dressing-table. The prospect of sliding his naked body between cool, crisply smooth sheets was disconcertingly alluring, given the fact that the only limbs waiting to enfold him there were the celibate arms of Morpheus. Perhaps he really *was* getting old!

He turned, a wry curve of self-derision on his lips, and froze.

The high, wide single bed was already occupied.

The pool of light spilling across the floor from the lamp behind him barely reached the blanket trailing off on to the floor but the general illumination was enough to show him that his crisp, tight, pristine sheets were a tangled memory. A woman lay sprawled on her stomach in his bed, one arm splayed across the rumpled sheet towards him, the other folded in at her side, her hand disappearing into the tawny froth of hair that rippled across her shoulders, glinting in the subdued light with the lustre of old gold. Her face was well and truly buried in one of Benedict's rare, private self-indulgences—the super-size down pillows with which he furnished his beds.

He closed his eyes and shook his head sharply, sure that what he saw must be a fatigue-induced hallucination.

He looked again, moving hesitantly towards the bed, still unwilling to trust the evidence of his weary, less than perfect eyesight.

As he got closer he could see the slow rise and fall of her back and hear the faint snuffle made by her breath on the pillow. She was definitely real.

Above the white cotton sheet which draped in modest folds over her hips and legs she wore a wisp of white satin, although judging from the turmoil of the rest of the bed any modesty was purely accidental. One thin white strap had straggled almost entirely off the arm tucked against her body and the consequent lop-sided sagging of white satin revealed a long, breathtaking sweep of graceful back sheathed in lustrously smooth-textured skin the colour of dark honey.

A powerful outrage gripped Benedict. It didn't even occur to his befuddled brain to question who she was; all he felt was a furious sense of betrayal. His precious privacy had been invaded!

This was *his* bed, *his* room, his *home*, God damn it! No matter that he had never called it such before, nor that it was only one of a number of residences he maintained.

And, hell, he was *tired*! All he wanted to do was sleep. Was that too much to ask in a man's own home?

Most infuriating of all was the fact that neither the shower nor the light had woken the feminine invader. Where he desperately longed to be she was already—fathoms deep in contented slumber. Well, not for long!

He bent over and growled savagely, 'Wake up, Goldilocks; Papa Bear wants his bed back.'

There was not a flicker of response. The allusion that had sprung unconsciously to his lips was ridiculously apposite, he thought as he straightened and glimpsed himself in the mirror of the dressing-table on the other side of the bed. Not only was he feeling emotionally bearish ... he was physically bare as well!

The little nip of sardonic humour restored a small measure of Benedict's normal equilibrium. He suddenly realised that waking up to find a stark-naked man looming over her was more likely to fling his mystery guest into hysterics than prompt a meek departure. The last thing his exhausted mind and body needed right now was to get involved in a dramatic scene.

He turned, intending to fetch his bathrobe from the hook in the bathroom, when the muted burr of his cellphone distracted him. Tired as he was he couldn't ignore the siren-call of master to technological slave. He detoured to his briefcase and pulled out the humming unit.

'So, are you home yet?'

Benedict raked his fingers over his cropped head as he recognised his friend and colleague's distinctive American drawl. 'Yes, Dane, *just*...and you won't believe what I found!'

A lazy chuckle that was Dane Judson's goodhumoured trademark vibrated in his ear. 'What do you think of her? Can I pick them, or what? Isn't she the most gorgeous thing you've ever seen?'

Benedict spun on his heel and stared incredulously at the woman on the bed. 'She—I—*you're* responsible for her being here?' he stuttered.

His friend laughed and Benedict could hear the faint clink of bottle against glass in the background. 'Uh-huh. Rendered you speechless, huh? I knew I'd do it one day. I just wish I could have been there to see your face, but I'm stuck here in Wellington until next week.'

'But what in the——?'

'Many happy returns for tomorrow, pal.' There was the audible sound of a toast being drunk.

Benedict cleared his throat as understanding burst upon his sluggish brain. 'This is your idea of a *birthday* present? For God's sake, Dane——!'

'Don't worry, pal, it's all pleasure and no responsibility,' Dane gleefully misunderstood him. 'You don't have to look after her for keeps—she's strictly on weekend loan. I promised you'd return her in perfect nick so make sure you treat her real lover-like——'

'*What*——?' Benedict moved jerkily back towards the bed, stunned by the revelation that the anonymous female body was there purely for his temporary delectation.

Another rolling laugh. 'I keep telling you, all work and no play makes Ben a dull boy. And don't tell me you're not feeling jaded because I know you well enough to read the signs. You need to revitalise yourself with a little hell-raising and, believe me, this babe is guaranteed to loosen you up real fast. A few days with her and you'll feel eighteen again...'

'I wouldn't wish a second time around as a teenager on my worst enemy,' Benedict said sardonically, unconsciously lowering his voice as he leaned against the bedside cabinet, wondering what Dane would say if he knew that his outrageous birthday present had got tired of waiting to spring her surprise and was out cold. Benedict decided not to spoil his friend's mirthful pleasure by telling him. 'Let alone my best friend. I hesitate to inject a dose of unwelcome reality into your adolescent fantasies, Dane, but isn't this kind of arrangement a bit unhealthy these days?'

Dane gave a whoop of delighted laughter. 'Afraid you'll have a heart-attack from the excitement? Come on, Ben—would I give you something that I thought would kill you? When was the last time you had some innocent, macho fun? A year? Eighteen months ago? Trust me, you have nothing to worry about. I had her thoroughly checked over inside *and* out and she's in prime, A-1 condition——'

'For God's sake——!' Benedict could feel the heat in his face, almost as if he was embarrassed on behalf of a woman who was obviously either a high-class call-girl or a free spirit who got her kicks out of having sex with total strangers. He knew it had been quite some time since his last relationship with a woman ended but he had been so absorbed in his work that he had never worried about his inactive libido. Not so Dane, it seemed, whose sex life was as active as his bizarre sense of humour.

'Dane——'

'No need to thank me, pal,' his friend interrupted, ringing off with a breezy, 'Just enjoy! And remember, it's pumpkin time Monday morning...'

Benedict swayed slightly under another rolling wave of fatigue as he switched off the phone and placed it clumsily down on the bedside table. He struggled to keep his eyelids open as he wearily debated his options.

There were plenty of other beds in the house but his proprietary interest in this one was stubbornly acute.

Despite her apparent sprawl, his nameless birthday gift actually trespassed on little more than half of the bed, he noted, her left arm and hip neatly aligned with the far edge of the single mattress. He looked down at her outflung arm, at the long, slender fingers curled laxly over the edge of the bed. Her fingertips almost touched his hair-roughened knee. Gently he encircled her wrist and lifted the sleep-heavy arm, placing it neatly back against her side. There was now an inviting expanse of empty bed available. A man-sized portion, if the man was of greyhound-lean proportions...

Goldilocks slumbered on. She was amazingly still, except for that slow, sensuous ripple of breath down the long, beautiful spine. She made sleep seem like an enchantingly erotic experience and Benedict found himself wondering whether a woman who offered herself up so voluptuously to sleep would be equally hedonistic in her approach to lovemaking.

A lazy stirring of male curiosity piqued his jaded senses, his angry earlier resentment overwhelmed by the knowledge that if he cared to find out he only needed to wake her. She was his to command. He wondered if that fleecy gold hair was as soft as it looked, and whether the colour was natural. He wondered whether her front would live up to that matchless back. Even in the slackness of sleep he could see that her muscles were well-toned. Her waking movements would be strong and supple. He imagined watching that golden back arching and flexing in slow, indolent rhythm with the languid thrust of his hips. He'd take her slow and easy at first... and then... and then...

He looked down at his quiescent body in rueful self-derision. And then... nothing. His mind might be aroused but he was so exhausted he was physically incapable of doing his vivid imagination justice. If he got into bed with her tonight he would be sleeping with her in the strictly literal sense.

Waking up with her in the morning, though, was suddenly an enchanting prospect.

Oh, yes... after a good, solid sleep the birthday boy would be in far better condition to appreciate his very unexpected, and undoubtedly expensive present...

CHAPTER TWO

VANESSA FLYNN was sitting at the scrubbed kitchen table sipping her first cup of coffee of the day when her employer burst into the kitchen and came to an abrupt halt.

Her hands tightened around the cup but that was the only visible reaction that escaped her rigid self-control. Inside she was one huge, all-enveloping blush.

Mrs Riley looked up from the breakfast tray she had busied herself over on the kauri-slab bench in surprise.

'Did you want your breakfast early this morning, Mr Savage?' she asked, her middle-aged face creased with dismay at this departure from routine. 'Only, your office never notified us that you were coming last night, you see, so nothing's quite prepared. I didn't even know that I'd be needed until Vanessa rang me a little while ago——'

'No, no...' Benedict Savage cut her off with a wave of his hand, frowning as he looked at the single setting she had laid on the tray. 'You don't have to rush.'

Vanessa braced herself as his gaze lifted, darted about the kitchen, and reluctantly settled on her.

She willed herself not to let her interior blush show, her dark brown eyes steady as they met his. She had dressed in her best wallpaper this morning—sensible, knee-length grey skirt and white short-sleeved blouse, her damp chestnut hair strictly confined to a neat French pleat, her face made up with the discreet foundation and barest touch of ginger lipstick that she habitually wore when on duty—too little to draw undue attention to her features but just enough to satisfy her feminine vanity.

14

Not that she had much reason to be vain. She was a shade under six feet but without the willowy slenderness that would have rendered her height fashionable. At least everything else was proportionate to her grand size, but that was little consolation. Her face was what might be politely termed strong-boned, her chin too square, her mouth too big and her wide, dark eyes deeply set and heavy-lidded, so that she was cursed with a perpetually sleepy air which was totally at odds with her practical efficiency.

She swallowed, the sweetened coffee turning bitter on her tongue as she withstood the silent stare of the man she had woken up in bed with that morning.

Behind the tortoiseshell frames she found his blue eyes unreadable. Not that Benedict Savage's expression was *ever* easy to interpret. To her he had always appeared as precise and controlled as the architectural drawings which papered the walls of the studio next to his bedroom.

He was also a very private man, reserved to the point of coldness. In fact it was that very reserve that made him an ideal employer as far as Vanessa was concerned ... that and the fact that his visits to his historic house on the east coast of the Coromandel Peninsula were few and far between, and *never* without advance notification.

Until now...

Vanessa's fingers tightened further on her cup. She had an unwelcome premonition that this visit was going to alter the pleasant tenor of life at Whitefield House completely and forever. Already her perception of Benedict Savage had been unwillingly altered. He was no longer merely her employer, he was now regrettably entrenched in her brain as a *man* ...

He was still looking at her, and she cringed at what he must be thinking.

If only she could remember what had happened!

Unfortunately, last night was a total blank, from the time she had fallen into bed after imbibing more than her share of champagne over an early dinner with Richard, until the moment she had become aware of the sounds of dawn filtering through a window that she knew she had firmly closed the previous evening.

When she had opened her eyes and found herself almost nose to nose with her naked employer, her arm draped over his hard waist, her thigh trapped intimately between his, she had thought at first that she was dreaming. Not that she had *ever* had erotic dreams about Benedict Savage before; she had always felt utterly safe in that regard. He was just not the sort of man she found attractive. He was too cerebral, too dispassionate, too much of a perfectionist for Vanessa, who much preferred comfort to sharp-edged perfection.

Luckily she had been too muddle-headed to scream when the rest of her senses had confirmed the shocking reality of the bare flesh pressed against hers. She had merely frozen, terrified that her consciousness might awaken his, unable to believe that the supple male hand possessively cupping her soft breast really belonged to Benedict Savage...not to mention the steely hardness that pressed into the hollow of her thigh where it was wedged snugly between his. He might not have roused from sleep but the man in her arms had definitely not been unaroused!

Shame and disbelief had warred for supremacy in the long moments it took for her to realise that she might still be able to extricate herself from the immediate consequences of her folly. The deep, even tenor of his breathing had indicated that Benedict—Mr Savage, she corrected herself grimly, clinging to the flimsy protection that the formality offered—was still deeply asleep, and Vanessa had prayed that he would continue to remain so as she extracted herself, inch by excruciatingly cautious inch, from their tangled embrace, her eyes fixed on his sleeping face.

All had gone well until the final few seconds when he'd shifted and growled an inarticulate protest at the withdrawal of warm, feminine flesh but, blessedly, he hadn't woken ...

When she'd finally slithered off the side of the bed, taking most of the upper sheet with her, he had merely rolled further over on to his face with a groan, slinging a long, sinewy arm around the pillow she had vacated and dragging it under his ribs, pinning it there with his drawn-up knee. She had primly flung the sheet back over him and fled hastily, her mortification ridiculously intensified by the knowledge that her presence in his bed was so easily replaced by a shapeless pillow!

It had taken her all of fifteen minutes' hard scrubbing in the shower to feel that she had washed the masculine scent and feel of him off her skin and even now the memory of it returned to haunt her.

Once again, she damned Benedict Savage for taking advantage of an innocent mistake. Why hadn't he woken her up? Or, worse, what if he *had* woken her and, in an alcohol-induced stupor, she had been recklessly wanton ... ?

She shuddered, looking warily up at him through the protective screen of her lashes. Why on earth was he just standing there like that? Why didn't he say something— an accusation, a joke, a request for an explanation, a demand she pack her bags and never darken his door again—*anything* to break this unbearable tension?

Nervously she tried to assess his uncertain mood. He hadn't shaved and his hair was ruffled—not a very good sign for a man who always presented a perfectly groomed image, even when relaxing in private. His saturnine face had a more than usually shuttered look, his thin mouth a tight slash across the unshaven lower half of his face that emphasised the general impression of indrawn tension. However, his crisp blue and white striped shirt and dark blue trousers were immaculately co-ordinated, so he hadn't been in such haste to track her down that he'd just thrown on the first clothes to hand.

The silence stretched on just long enough for her nerve to break under the strain.

'Did you want me, sir?'

Too late Vanessa realised the suggestive ambiguity of the question and she had to clench her teeth to stop herself gabbling a disclaimer into the ensuing silence. Her neatly buttoned collar suddenly felt chokingly tight.

'I . . .' He released her from the torture of his sole attention, looking around the kitchen again, as if hunting for his words. 'Er... Am I the only one breakfasting...?'

Vanessa was aware of Mrs Riley's sidelong glance but refused to share her silent puzzlement at their employer's uncharacteristic vagueness. She was too busy worrying over whether he was deliberately prolonging her agony or merely unwilling to humiliate her in front of the housekeeper.

'Why... yes. Vanessa didn't mention that you'd brought any guests with you this time...' Mrs Riley was saying, a faint look of bewilderment crossing her face as she watched her employer's eyes drop as he studied his stylishly shod feet with apparent fascination.

'No, I didn't. So... it's just me, then...' His inflexion rose slightly on the last word, just enough to suggest the possibility of a question. Nobody answered immediately and his gaze swivelled suddenly back to Vanessa, who wasn't quite quick enough to banish her look of apprehension.

He scowled at her. 'Can I see you for a few minutes in the library, Flynn?' He turned on his heel and was almost out the door before he halted, looking back. 'Incidentally, Mrs Riley, I'm really not very hungry this morning, so perhaps just some toast and tea...'

'Oh, what a pity, Mr Savage, and I've just put a nice pot of porridge on the stove——'

'*Porridge*?' He jerked around, looking so shocked at the suggestion that Vanessa, already primed with nerves, gave a jittery little laugh and found herself once again impaled by the focus of his attention.

'In the library. Now!' For Benedict Savage the quiet hiss was the equivalent of a furious shout.

'Yes, sir!' Vanessa muttered to empty air, rising from her seat and unhooking the cropped navy jacket that was draped over the high back.

'Well, I never!' said Kate Riley, crossing her arms over her ample chest and shaking her grey head so that her corrugated perm quivered. 'You'd have thought I was offering him arsenic. He always said he liked my porridge!'

Vanessa, shouldering into her jacket and procrastinating by squaring the cuffs and lapels, soothed her injured pride absently. 'He's probably just in a bad mood——'

'Mr Savage doesn't have moods—he's always a perfect gentleman,' Mrs Riley pointed out with inescapable truth. 'He never gets out of bed on the wrong side but it certainly seems as though he did this morning...'

Vanessa murmured something indistinct in answer to the unfortunate metaphor and rushed out of the kitchen, pressing cold hands to her hot cheeks.

Calm down, calm down, she lectured herself sternly as she walked down the flag-stoned hall. If he fires you, you can charge him with sexual harassment. Or was he planning to charge *her* . . . ? She almost moaned aloud at the thought, its absurdity eclipsed by her horror of scandal. Whatever happened, there would be questions asked because she couldn't possibly continue to work at Whitefield. She would have to leave the place she had come to look on as a quiet, secure haven from the madness of the world. And what was she going to tell Richard? Oh, damn, damn, *damn*!

'Well...?' Thankfully Benedict Savage had not chosen to adopt an intimidating position of dominance behind the meticulously tidy antique desk that fronted the French windows. Instead he was standing just inside the doorway, one hand resting on a walnut shelf of the book-lined wall, fingers tapping involuntarily against the aged wood as she closed the door behind her.

'Yes, sir?' Vanessa stood straight and tall, shoulders squared against the imminent attack.

He cleared his throat. 'I'm sorry if my early arrival has caused problems, but I just needed to get away for a space of time and Whitefield seemed the place to do it. The apartment in Auckland is too accessible and...' he shrugged with a trace of diffidence '...well, I know that Mrs Riley gets in a tizz about these things... Just make sure she knows that I don't expect everything to be as organised as usual...that I don't want any fuss...'

Vanessa was hard put to it not to let her jaw fall open. Mr Perfection was telling her he didn't expect per-fection? He was waffling about household arrangements when the real business at hand was shrieking to be settled?

She looked at the tapping fingers. Nerves? Mr Cool was *nervous*?

'So, you'll tell her that, will you?' His fingers sud-denly stopped their fluttering with a sudden slam against the wood.

Vanessa's eyes shot back to his face to find him watching her warily. She scrabbled for foundation on a rapidly shifting ground. *He* was nervous of *her*? The notion was mind-boggling.

'Ah, yes, yes, of course, sir,' she assured him hastily.

'Right.' He took off his spectacles, cleaned their spotless lenses with a beautifully pressed handkerchief

retrieved from his hip pocket, and put them on again.
'I didn't bring anyone with me.'

'So you said, sir—in the kitchen, just now,' she added
as he regarded her blankly.

'Did I? Oh, yes, of course I did.' He pushed off the
bookcase and began to pace. 'So...where is our other
guest, I wonder?'

Vanessa stiffened. 'If you're suggesting——'

He jumped in, correspondingly quick to suspect.
'Suggesting what?'

'That I take advantage of your absences to invite
people to use your house——' she began, angry that he
might be trying to make up spurious reasons for
terminating her employment. If he was going to fire her
for sleeping with him he was going to have to admit it!

'No, no, nothing like that.' His answer was as swift
as it seemed genuine, and edged with irritation. 'If I
didn't trust you I wouldn't continue to employ you,
would I? I just wondered if you knew...'

'Knew what?' She was deeply uneasy now. Maybe she
just should have opened up with an apology and explanation instead of leaving it up to him to introduce the
subject. But she had never known her employer be anything but direct, sometimes brutally so.

He stopped pacing a mere stride away and turned to
her, hands on his hips. This was it, the moment of truth.

Vanessa lifted her chin bravely, gratified to note that
even in flat heels she topped him by at least an inch.
Whatever he said, she wasn't going to shrink into physical
insignificance before him!

'There was a woman...'

'A woman?' Vanessa felt herself beginning to heat up.
Oh, God, was he going to try to smooth things over by
explaining how last night had only been a spasm of lust
and that she wasn't to place any importance on the fact
that they had slept together because there was
someone else...?

He bit off something that sounded like a curse. Another first. Benedict Savage's words were usually as cool and as measured as the rest of him, precisely weighed and placed for maximum effect with minimum effort.

'Yes, a woman.' His voice roughened sharply at her wide-eyed shock and he raked her with an insulting glare. 'You *do* know what a woman is, don't you, Flynn?'

Her flush deepened at his sneer and she saw his eyes flicker behind their clear lenses, his mouth compress with self-disgust. 'I'm sorry, that was in extremely poor taste...' His hand rasped across his beard-shaded chin as he continued rigidly, 'I mean...last night when I came in, just before midnight...there was a woman—er—in my room...'

'In your room?' She couldn't help it, and when she realised that she had once again inanely repeated his words she bit her lip but this time he ignored the provocation.

'In bed. A blonde.'

'A *blonde*?' Vanessa retreated, startled, visions of sin dancing in her head. Had she taken part in some kind of orgy without being aware of it? Disported herself in some kind of perverted *ménage à trois*? Her employer had never brought a female companion with him to Whitefield before, although he had included unattached women in groups of people whom he had occasionally entertained at weekends. She had thought that his love-life must be as reserved as the rest of him, but now Vanessa found herself regarding those weekend groupings in a suspicious new light.

'Oh, for God's sake!' Her air of silent condemnation caused an explosion that was contained almost as soon as it occurred. His hard jaw clenched as he continued doggedly, 'She had long, fluffy hair...like golden fleece.' Benedict Savage held her mesmerised stare, faint streaks of red appearing on his high cheekbones as he went on,

'Have you by any chance seen her around this morning? She's not anywhere upstairs...'

Golden? *Fluffy*? Vanessa's eyes widened as she resisted the urge to touch her neat French pleat to make sure that the wavy, sun-bleached ends were firmly rolled into the concealing centre.

It suddenly occurred to her that her employer had never seen her with her hair down. To him she was just Flynn, discreet, sexless, quietly running his household and overseeing the ongoing restoration of the former coaching inn while he jaunted about the world earning a luxurious living designing buildings that were the complete antithesis of Whitefield.

Vanessa, along with the other permanent staff, was merely one of the chattels that he had acquired when he had unexpectedly inherited a distant relative's property and, after initially balking badly at the discovery that the late Judge Seaton's butler was young and female, he had accepted the impeccable references supplied by the lawyer who had handled the judge's estate. He had, however, made it quite clear to Vanessa privately that she was only acceptable in the position as long as the fact that she was a woman never impinged on the job. It never had.

'Apart from being blonde, what does she look like?' Vanessa asked in a strangled voice that tested a wildly implausible theory.

'I don't know,' he said, his bluntness daring her to display any shock. 'It was dark... I never saw her face. And before you ask, no, I don't know what her name is; we didn't get around to introducing ourselves! So, now that your prurient suspicions are confirmed, perhaps you wouldn't mind answering *my* questions?'

His sarcasm went right over her whirling head. She was shattered by knowledge that her outrageous theory was right.

There had only been one woman in Benedict Savage's bed last night and that woman had been Vanessa. But he didn't know that!

'I . . . but . . . I——' Relief poured like adrenalin along her veins, throwing her into an even deeper moral dilemma.

As long as he never found out who the woman in his bed had been, Vanessa's job was safe . . .

'I'm not imagining things!' he growled tersely.

Vanessa licked her lips. 'Oh . . . of course not,' she said, wondering how long her meagre acting skills would sustain her charade of ignorance.

He chose to take her placating comment as a piece of sarcasm and reiterated tightly, 'She was here, damn it! It was late and I was thick-headed with jet-lag but I wasn't *completely* detached from reality. I *wasn't* hallucinating!'

'I haven't seen anyone except Mrs Riley this morning,' Vanessa said, carefully avoiding any outright lie that could have unpleasant repercussions later. 'Perhaps it was one of the resident ghosts, sir,' she joked weakly.

'I didn't know we had any. Not that I believe in them, anyway.'

His scepticism was only what she expected from such a logical mind. You only had to look at the buildings he designed to see that his imagination was chained to the starkly realistic. 'Oh, yes, people say that there are several——'

'Female?'

She was disconcerted by his persistence over what had been a purely frivolous mention. 'A couple of them, yes——'

'Yellow-haired? Scantily dressed? A seductive siren luring a man towards the gates of hell and damnation?'

Oh, God, now she was *certain* that whatever they had got up to had been deeply sinful.

'Er, I understand one of them was a guest murdered by one of the ostlers here at the inn—a...a dancing girl who was on her way to entertain at the goldfields at Coromandel...'

'You mean a whore?' He cut her gentle euphemisms to ribbons with cool contempt. 'Well, that certainly fits.'

'There's no proof that she was a whore!' Vanessa said hotly, not sure whether it was herself or the ghost she was supposed to be defending.

'What about last night?'

'W-what about last night?' Vanessa quavered. Surely she hadn't given him the idea she had expected money for whatever it was she had allowed him to do!

He looked at her impatiently, mistaking her horror for fear. 'Forget about bloody ghosts. They don't exist. So-called supernatural apparitions usually turn out to be the self-generated fantasies of people who are either gullible, publicity-seeking or deranged. You said you didn't see anyone around this morning. What about last night? You were here then, weren't you? Did you see or hear anything then?'

Oh, God... Her collar tightened again, squeezing her voice into a reedy squeak. 'I was out. I went to dinner over in Waihi...' No need to mention she'd been back, and tucked up cosily in his bed, by ten-thirty p.m.

'Who with?'

In the three years she had worked for him he had never asked her a single personal question and Vanessa floundered, feeling that she was giving away a vital piece of herself with the information. 'R-Richard—Richard Wells.'

'The horse-breeder—from the property along the road?' He frowned. He was obviously trying to re-member his fleeting acquaintance with his nearest neighbour; he was probably also wondering what Richard saw in his sexless employee, Vanessa thought sourly, only to be proved wrong as he said sharply, 'Not with Dane?'

Vanessa gasped. 'Mr Judson? Of course not. As far as I know he's at home in Auckland.'

'Wellington, actually. So he didn't tell you about his little arrangement...' He resumed his pacing, looking slightly more relaxed, but Vanessa couldn't allow her vigilance to relax correspondingly.

'Arrangement?'

'It doesn't matter.' He glanced out of the French doors towards the back of the house and suddenly halted with a jerk. 'What the——? Whose car is that in the garage?'

Desperate for a change of subject, Vanessa moved up beside him to look out at the gleaming white car tucked under the open arches of what had once been the coaching-house stables. 'Oh, that! It——'

'What an incredibly beautiful beast of a car!' His envious drawl cut her off, startling her with its hint of boyish eagerness. Benedict Savage, the last word in sophistication—*boyish*? 'Isn't it a——?' He leaned closer to the glass panes. 'Yes, I think it is...a 1935 Duesenberg convertible coupé...just like the one Clark Gable had custom-made. Who on earth...?' He straightened, suddenly letting loose a rare laugh that sounded half annoyed, half admiring. 'My God, I bet *she* arrived in it! That would just be Dane's style. So that must mean she's still here somewhere——'

Vanessa stared at him, confused by this added complication. 'But...I thought it was *yours*.'

His head snapped sideways. 'Mine?' His eyebrows rose in a haughty disclaimer. 'What on earth gave you that idea? You know very well I have the BMW.'

Yes, a precision-engineered, elegantly low-key car that had seemed perfectly suited to his introverted personality. And yet here he was, practically drooling over a flashy, red-upholstered brute whose every gleaming inch was flauntingly extrovert.

'Well ... I ... it was delivered yesterday in your name, so I naturally assumed... I thought perhaps you'd bought it as an investment...' It was the only explanation that had fitted his coolly calculating image.

'It was delivered? By whom?' As usual he cut swiftly to the heart of the matter.

'Two men. Yesterday afternoon. There was a letter— I assumed from the dealer. I put it there on your desk with the car keys.'

With one last, narrow-eyed glance at the car he picked up the flat envelope and slit the sealed edge with a neatly manicured thumbnail.

What he withdrew wasn't a letter, but a large card of some kind. He stared at the weedy-looking, spectacle-wearing nerd that Vanessa, pretending not to look but unable to restrain her curiosity, could see gracing the front, before slowly opening it and reading the contents. As Vanessa watched, the flush that had lightly streaked his skin a few minutes earlier exploded into a full-blooded, Technicolor blush. He made a strange choking sound in his throat.

Vanessa was fascinated. She had never seen him look so flustered. 'I beg your pardon, sir?' she murmured, her determined coolness rewarded by his dazed regard.

'Dane's given me a *car*...'

'*Given* you a car?' She now understood his helpless amazement. She had known that his friend was wealthy, as were most people professionally associated with her employer, but, even as ignorant about cars as Vanessa was, she realised that the gorgeous specimen in the garage was worth hundreds of thousands of dollars. Dane Judson had a quirky sense of humour and a liking for extravagant surprises, but his extravagances had never been reckless.

'For my birthday.' He scanned the card again and corrected himself. 'No, not given, *loaned*—it's being picked up again on Monday...'

That was more like it. Quirky but grounded in economic reality!

'It's your birthday?' For some reason Vanessa had never thought of her employer having birthdays like ordinary people. He had always been so remote as to be ageless, above such frivolous goings-on as birthdays...

'Today. I'm thirty-four,' he revealed absently, staring down at the card, reading and re-reading the writing inside as if it were printed in a foreign language that he was having difficulty translating.

'Many happy returns,' Vanessa murmured weakly, wishing she had some recollection of the precise nature of the gift *she* had rendered on the eve of his birthday.

He didn't respond, raking a hand over his head, spiking up more of the ruffled strands.

'My God, last night on the phone...all that time Dane was talking about lending me a *car*, and *I* thought he was talking in clever metaphors...'

He groaned and closed his appalled eyes. 'My God, if he ever finds out what I thought I'll never hear the end of it!' His hand covered his mouth as he groaned again, with heartfelt disgust, and his next mutter was almost smothered. 'I must be mad! Ghosts? I could have *sworn* I hadn't imagined any of it...'

'Why, what *did* you think he was giving you?' Vanessa asked, the extreme nature of his reaction spicing her curiosity.

His hand dropped away, and the eyes that had been blue with dismay chilled to the colour of pure steel, but his complexion was still betrayingly warm. 'None of your damned business!'

She knew then exactly what 'arrangement' he thought that his sly-humoured friend had made.

She pokered up immediately, forcing down a rush of humiliated fury at the thought of being used as a sexual birthday favour. At least she had the excuse of being inebriated for whatever licentiousness she might have indulged in. He had no excuse whatsoever! And he hadn't even bothered to look at her *face*! Her woman's body had been all that had mattered. Her normally placid temper simmered dangerously.

'No, sir.'

His eyes narrowed on her, as if he sensed the insolence she so badly wanted to display, but she remained stubbornly impassive and with a shrug he picked up the car keys, tossing and catching them in a gesture that was subtly defiant. 'I think I'll go and check out this magnanimous gift of Dane's.'

'I'll tell Mrs Riley to hold your breakfast,' said Vanessa smoothly as she watched him open the French doors and slip outside.

She knew what he was doing and a small smile of malicious satisfaction curved along her wide mouth.

The imperturbable Benedict Savage was running away. She had witnessed the temporary disintegration of his cynical self-possession and that made him uncomfortable. He knew that she was a shrewd judge of human behaviour—it was what made her such a skilled butler, responsive to the needs of him and his guests to the extent that she seemed able to anticipate their every wish—and he had no desire to be judged on his vulnerabilities. Until now he had been serene in the knowledge that his was the dominant role in the master-servant relationship and now it had probably occurred to him that that balance of power wasn't immutable, that the power of knowledge accumulated over time might make a servant of the master.

Good! It would serve him right to wonder how much she knew or might guess. She hoped he would relive his discomfort every time he saw her for some time to come. Why shouldn't he suffer at least a modicum of the helpless self-consciousness that *she* felt in his presence?

She watched him cross the cobbled courtyard that led to the stables with a smooth, lean-hipped stride, keenly aware of a unique feeling of alienation within her own body and fiercely resenting it. Suddenly she wished that she hadn't been too embarrassed to inspect the body she had briskly scrubbed under the shower an hour ago. Whatever had happened in his bed might have left marks, evidence that might have relieved her fears—or confirmed them—instead of leaving her in this limbo of . . .

Evidence?

Give that fearsomely logical brain physical evidence to work on and she wouldn't stand a chance!

She stiffened, her heart fluttering in her chest. A fresh surge of panic galvanised her into action. She darted over to the French doors and turned the key in the lock before racing out into the hallway and up the stairs, taking them three at a time, her long legs comfortably stretching the distance.

The door to her employer's bedroom was firmly shut but Vanessa ignored any qualms she had about invading his privacy and skidded inside.

The bed was in exactly the state that she had fervently hoped it would be—abandoned and very much unmade. Vanessa blessed the fact that Benedict Savage's parents had raised him in a rich and rarefied environment that rendered him ignorant of the kind of basic domestic chores that ordinary mortals like Vanessa grew up performing for themselves.

She quickly ripped the top sheet off the bed, rolling it into a loose ball before dumping it on the floor and attacking the pillows, cursing their ungainly size as she struggled to remove the custom-made pillowcases. Her heart pounded as she spotted the long strands on hair that straggled across one of them. She had never realised that she moulted so much at night . . . or had it been because this time her head had been thrashing to and fro on the pillow in the throes of unremembered ecstasy?

Her mouth went dry at the insidious image of herself writhing beneath a sleekly tapered male body. Who would have thought that under the fashionably loose clothes a man in a sedentary occupation like architectural design would have a body so hard and compact? His skin had been glossy with health, rippling over lean, surprisingly well-developed muscles.

Furious with herself for letting her thoughts run riot, Vanessa wrenched anew at the stubborn pillowcases and shook them out vigorously before turning them inside out and throwing them on top of the sheet on the floor. She stretched across the bed and had just slipped her hand under the mattress to free the far corner of the sheet when the door jarred open, and a voice rattled chills down her spine.

'What in the hell do you think you're doing?'

She could feel one neatly manicured nail catch and tear against the mattress as she jerked upright and around, her sensible shoes skidding on the discarded linen, tangling her feet, so that with a cry of dismay she toppled helplessly backwards across the bed.

CHAPTER THREE

ANYONE else would have reflexively reached out and tried to prevent Vanessa's fall, but Benedict Savage was a law unto himself. He didn't lift a finger to save her.

He merely folded his arms across his chest and watched her bounce and come to rest before coldly rephrasing his question.

'I asked you what you were doing in my room?'

The crisp pattern of his speech was slightly blurred by his rapid breathing. He had been running. What had occurred to her had obviously also belatedly occurred to him; he was here to attempt to sort fact from fantasy.

If she had felt at a disadvantage earlier in his study, it was nothing to what Vanessa felt now.

She pushed herself upright on trembling arms, drawing her knees together and tugging down the skirt over her dangling legs in a vain attempt to recover her dignity. 'I would have thought it was obvious,' she snapped defensively, wishing he would move out of the way so that she could stand up. 'I'm making your bed.'

'Why?'

She bit back the smart-mouthed reply that sprang to her lips and struggled for a respectful monotone. 'Because it's my job.'

'*You* make my bed?'

For a moment he looked as uncomfortable as she felt. He had refused to allow her to perform the more personal services that a butler usually provided, ones that she had cheerfully carried out for the judge—waking him in the morning, running his bath, laying out his choice of clothing for the day. Benedict Savage had informed her squelchingly at that chilly initial interview that he didn't require nannying, and that he would thank her not to invade his privacy unless invited. She had duly kept the required distance, but it wouldn't hurt him to realise that caring for someone's house was, in its own way, as intimate as caring for their person.

'I often help Mrs Riley with the housekeeping,' she said, adding pointedly, 'As you may have noticed from the household accounts, I only employ extra housekeeping staff when you bring guests to stay. It's not economic to have a full household complement idle for most of the year.'

His blank look confirmed a long-held suspicion. She doubted that he ever bothered even to glance at the accounts that she scrupulously presented him with every six months. She could be robbing him blind for all he cared. Once he had decided to trust her, he had given her a totally free hand and however flattering that was to her ego it irked her that it also meant the true extent of her efficiency went largely unappreciated.

Unfortunately he ignored the red herring, and pursued a point she had hoped would not occur to such a supremely undomesticated animal.

'Have I ever given you reason to think I'm so fanatical about cleanliness that I require my sheets to be changed daily?' he said drily. 'This is a home, not a hotel—I've barely had the chance to get them warm, let alone dirty.'

'You do have a reputation for being extremely fastidious,' Vanessa muttered, guiltily thinking of the silky heat that she had been cuddled up to that morning. He had certainly been warming the sheets then. However, she could hardly contradict him.

'But not to the point of being unhealthily obsessive,' he said with controlled distaste.

No, she couldn't picture him being obsessive about anything. That would require a degree of passion she didn't believe he possessed.

'You haven't been here since the beginning of February and your bed hasn't been properly aired because we didn't know you were coming,' she invented hastily. 'I thought the sheets might have been a bit musty.'

'Well, they weren't.' He looked down at the tumble of linen at their feet, his voice acquiring a strangely husky note. 'In fact they were quite deliciously fragrant...'

Vanessa tensed with shock at the thread of remembered pleasure in his voice, finding his choice of words disturbingly sensual for someone whom she preferred to think of as a thoroughly cold fish.

Thank God the perfume she had dabbed on at the beginning of last evening was so expensive that she only wore it when she was going somewhere special! She sought for a way to scatter whatever images were reforming in that frighteningly intelligent brain.

'Probably from the washing-powder Mrs Riley uses,' she said prosaically, and rose from the bed, forcing him to step back as she summoned a brisk dismissal.

'Well, since I've gone this far I'll have to finish the job. I can't put these sheets back on after they've been trampled on the floor. Excuse me.'

He looked from the bed to her and for a terrible moment she thought he was going to dig his heels in. She bravely stood her ground, banking on his intensely private nature to win the brief internal battle he was evidently waging. The thought of exposing himself to her curiosity again would be anathema to him. She deliberately allowed a hint of speculation to impinge on her expression of polite patience.

His reaction was swift and instinctive. His face shuttered and he inclined his head, saying sharply, 'If you think it's necessary, I suppose I must bow to your superior domestic knowledge.'

Sarcastic beast! In the past his cynical comments hadn't bothered her. Now every word he uttered seemed to grate on her nerves.

'Thank you.' She hesitated, waiting for him to depart. He looked at her enquiringly, raising his dark eyebrows haughtily above his spectacle frames. It had the irritating effect of making Vanessa feel as if he was looking down on her, even though the reverse was true. She had won their little tussle of wills and now she was being made to pay for it.

Vanessa's wide mouth pinched as she strove for the self-effacing politeness that until this morning had been second nature in her dealings with this man.

'I'm sure you must have something better to do than watch me make beds.'

'Not really,' he said unobligingly. 'When you're on holiday there's something very satisfying about watching other people toil.'

'You're on holiday?' Vanessa hoped she didn't sound as appalled as she felt. He had never spent more than a long weekend at Whitefield before. Surely he wasn't staying any longer than Sunday? She didn't think she could take the strain.

An idle Benedict Savage would undoubtedly be a bored Benedict Savage, and when bored he might look around for something to engage his intellect—like solving a puzzle that was best left unsolved.

To hide her agitation Vanessa gave the remaining sheet a huge yank to free it and rolled it clumsily up over her arm.

'More or less,' he replied absently, watching her bend to pick up the rest of the linen. 'You could say I'm in between jobs at the moment.'

She was so used to hearing that euphemistic phrase trotted out by people who came to the door applying for casual work, thinking that domestic service was a sinecure for which they needed no skill, training or enthusiasm, that her soothing response was automatic, her mind occupied with more weighty matters.

'I'm sure you'll find other employment again soon.'

'I'm flattered by your confidence. But if not I suppose there's always the unemployment benefit.' His smooth answer followed so seamlessly on hers that it was a moment before she realised her *faux pas*.

'I'm sorry, sir, I wasn't thinking,' she said, mortified by her slip.

'I thought it was the reverse,' he murmured with dismaying perception, his blue eyes studying her flustered face. 'You seemed to be very deeply immersed in uneasy thoughts. Is there anything worrying you, Flynn?'

Another unprecedented personal question. Now was the moment to confess all and throw herself on his mercy!

Only Vanessa didn't think that he had any. She vividly recalled his declaration at their meeting that he never made an idle threat and she had seen him deal ruthlessly with those who proved to be dishonest or disloyal. Employee or friend, they simply ceased to exist for him. Vanessa was already in over her head in deceit and, in addition, she had broken his golden rule: thou shalt not be a woman.

'No, why should you think that?' Unfortunately her voice cracked on the last word.

'There's a slightly...fraught air about you this morning.'

Oh, God!

'Is there?' she said brightly. 'Well, your arrival did rather catch me on the hop.' She was glad of the ready excuse. 'I'm afraid I don't react well to surprises.'

'Really? Congreve would have it that uncertainty is one of the joys of life,' he said suavely, no doubt trying to intimidate her with his intellect. Well, Vanessa wasn't impressed. Anyone who could read could trot out quotations from classic English literature. She might not have gone to university but she could, and did, love to read widely. With anyone else she might even have enjoyed a foolish game of duelling quotations. As it was she just wanted him to find her dull and boring and totally unworthy of his interest.

'Not mine,' said Vanessa firmly, starting to edge towards the door, clutching her burden. She didn't trust this sudden communicativeness of his. He had never shown any inclination to discuss literature or philosophy with his butler before...or 'household executive assistant' as he had ludicrously suggested she be re-titled.

She had given that idea short shrift. She was a butler and proud of it. It was what she had trained for. It was in her blood. Her English father was a butler and she had grown up in the stately British household that was his fiefdom, fascinated by the day-to-day management of what was not only a home but a family seat, and a three-hundred-year-old one at that. It had been her fond ambition to hold a similar position one day but, as she had discovered, life had a nasty way of subverting youthful ambitions.

'No? That surprises me. I thought that coping with the unexpected was one of your great strengths. You certainly never had any problem accommodating the most bizarre requests of my guests... You didn't turn a hair at the pet lion cub, or the demand to find enough sculls for a wagered boat race on the lake, or, for that matter, the man who collapsed in the soup with a newly developed seafood allergy. Without your prompt action he might have died.'

'I didn't say I couldn't cope,' said Vanessa, taken aback by his easy recall of incidents she had assumed were long dismissed from his mind as supremely unimportant. At the time they occurred she had merely received a cool word of approval, as if she had done nothing more, nor less, than was required of her. 'I just said I didn't react well—personally, I mean. I get churned up inside...'

'It doesn't show.'

'Thank you.' She was already regretting having told him that much. He was studying her with an intentness that increased her anxieties.

Her fingers curled into her palms as she fought the desire to check her hair. As it dried it would lighten several shades to the warm caramel that was so susceptible to the bleaching effects of the summer sun, although thankfully the gel she used to keep the sides tidy would prevent its waviness becoming too obvious. Still, Benedict Savage was an architect, skilled in the interpretation of line and form, observant of small details that might escape others...

'It was a comment, not a compliment.'

'In my profession that *is* a compliment,' Vanessa retorted with an unconscious air of smugness that prompted an amused drawl.

'Being a servant is hardly one of the professions.'

Vanessa bristled at the implied slur. Snob!

'Of course not, sir. I humbly beg your pardon for my presumption, sir.' She would have bowed and tugged her forelock but that would be going over the top. As it was his eyes glinted dangerously.

'You have a devastating line in obsequiousness, Flynn. One might almost suspect it was insolence. Why have I never noticed that before, I wonder?'

Because she had never allowed herself to be so fixed in his attention before. Aghast at her foolishness, Vanessa tried to retrench.

'I don't mean to be——'

'You mean you didn't think I'd notice. Have I really been so complacent an employer?'

'No, of course not,' she lied weakly, and watched his thin mouth crook in a faint sneer.

'Sycophancy, Flynn? Was that on the curriculum at that exclusive English school for butlers that you graduated, drenched with honours, from?'

This fresh evidence of the acuteness of his memory was daunting. She hugged the trailing sheets to her chest and refused to answer, realising that no answer, however cunningly phrased, would please him. He didn't *want* to be pleased. He wanted a whipping-boy for his frustration. The irony was that she had richly earned the position!

'That's right,' he said silkily. 'Humour me. After all, you can afford to. You know I can't fire you.'

'Can't you?' Vanessa said, sensing an unforeseen trap in his goading.

'Well, I could, but that would jeopardise all that I'm doing here, wouldn't it?'

'Would it?' Vanessa was now bewildered.

'You could tie me up in legal manoeuvring for years——'

'Could I?'

Her response was a little too quick, a little too curious. His eyes narrowed. Vanessa straightened her spine and squared her shoulders, lifting her chin in a characteristic attempt to establish her physical superiority.

'I could, couldn't I?' she rephrased with a suitable tinge of menace, but not all the threatening body language and fighting language at her disposal could redeem that brief and telling hesitation.

'Could you?'

'Yes.' Her teeth nibbled unknowingly at her full lower lip.

'And how, precisely, would you do it?'

She was even more at sea, the look in his blue eyes creating a turbulence that reminded her what a poor sailor she was. He looked amused and—her stomach roiled—almost *compassionate*!

'Well, I . . . I . . .'

'You don't know, do you?' he said gently. 'You have absolutely no idea what I'm talking about.'

She lifted her chin even higher. 'No.' Her tone implied that neither did she care to find out.

He knew better.

'Did you not understand Judge Seaton's lawyer when he explained the situation to you?' he said, still with that same, infuriating gentleness. 'He assured me that he'd spoken to you directly after the funeral and that you'd appeared quite calm and collected.'

Vanessa frowned, trying to remember, her brows rumpling her smooth, wide forehead.

She had looked on Judge Seaton as not only a saviour but also as a man she had respected and admired and come to develop a fond affection for.

He had rescued her from the depths of misfortune and she, in turn, had travelled across the world with him, rescuing him from the inertia of his unwelcome retirement and the vicissitudes of old age and an irascible personality. Solitary by nature and never having married, when the judge had started having difficulty in getting about and suffering short memory lapses Vanessa had been the one who chivvied him out of his fits of depression and inspired him to start the book he had still been enthusiastically working on when he died—a social history of his adopted home, Whitefield House, and the surrounding Coromandel region.

His death, though not unexpected in view of his failing health, had been a shock, and at the time of the funeral Vanessa had still been numb and subconsciously hostile towards any threat of change in the haven that she had striven to create for herself at Whitefield. She had mentally switched off at any mention of an arrogantly youthful usurper who, it seemed to her, was proposing to take up his inheritance with unconscionable speed, given the fact that he had never bothered to visit his benefactor while he was alive, nor deigned to attend his funeral.

When Benedict Savage had finally made his appearance a week later he had proved totally alien to the late judge both physically and in temperament—something else that Vanessa had fiercely resented.

The fact that the hostility between them was mutual had suited her preconceptions so well that she had sought no explanation for it beyond the superficial. She was safe with male hostility. She could deal with it. It was male interest that made her nervous—self-consciously clumsy, inept and, worst of all, frighteningly vulnerable.

'I remember him rambling on and on about the will,' she said slowly. 'About there being no financial provision for me or some such thing, not that I expected one—I wasn't family and I'd only been with him two years. I don't remember what the lawyer said exactly. I was tired; I wasn't concentrating very well. I was the one who had to make all the arrangements for the funeral, you know. You didn't bother to arrive until it was all over!' There was a touch of querulousness in her voice, the echo of that three-year-old hostility.

'I won't apologise for that,' he said evenly. 'George Seaton and I were only very distantly related on my mother's side. He may well have not known of my existence—I certainly didn't know of his. He didn't leave the house to me by name, he simply deeded it to his closest surviving male blood-relative. Needless to say, my mother was *not* amused at being told she was no more than a mere twig on the family inheritance tree.'

She hadn't known that. It certainly threw a different light on his behaviour. And, having found his parents, on the strength of their single, fleeting visit to Whitefield, even more frigid, hypercritical and self-orientated than their son, she could just imagine Denise Savage's classically beautiful face frozen in an expression of Victorian

affront at being confronted with the evidence of her un-
importance in the male scheme of things.

A ghost of a smile widened Vanessa's mouth. 'He was
an appalling old male chauvinist pig,' she admitted with
affectionate disapproval.

'And yet he hired a female butler barely out of her
teens?'

For once Vanessa didn't freeze up at the delicate probe.

'I just happened to be in the right place at the right
time.' And for all the wrong reasons, extremely sordid
ones. 'His previous butler had died after being with him
for about fifty years. I don't think he could bear the
idea of setting another man in his place and I suppose
I appealed to his sense of chivalry...'

'Why do you say that?'

Her mouth twisted softly awry. 'He felt sorry for
me——' She had almost forgotten whom she was talking
to but a sudden shift in his alertness, causing light to
flash like a warning signal off the lenses of his glasses,
reminded her. 'I was in between jobs at the time,' she
explained blandly.

'Well, he certainly made sure you wouldn't lose this
one,' Benedict commented. 'A condition of my inheriting
was that I retain the services of the existing butler for
at least five years from the date of probate being
granted...unless said butler voluntarily relinquished her
duties.'

Vanessa's eyes and mouth rounded in astonishment at
the revelation. Then a rush of anger flushed her system
and her mouth snapped. 'But that first day—you
threatened to get rid of me because I was a woman!'

'Untrue. I simply suggested that you would not find
me as congenial as the judge to work for, and that you
would be happier elsewhere. And I think that "girl"
might have been the word I actually used...'

'Suggested nothing! You were deliberately insulting,'
Vanessa remembered bitterly. 'You implied I couldn't

do the job because of my sex. You implied that I only had it because I had some kind of hold over a senile old man. The judge wasn't senile and you knew it—the lawyer must have been perfectly clear about the validity of that will. You were trying to get me to quit!' she realised explosively. 'Well, I'm glad I refused!'

Not for the world would she tell him that it was cowardice that had held her back, not a determination to prove him wrong. Not even his slimy allegations could winkle her out of the safe little burrow she had dug for herself. Whitefield needed her and she needed Whitefield. Here she was known only by her name and her job, and not by her reputation.

'And I wasn't a girl, either!' she finished angrily, determined to deny him on all counts. 'I was twenty, and I've always been very mature for my age.' It was what had been her downfall—her air of calm self-sufficiency combined with a body that, Everest-like, was a challenge to a particular kind of man simply because it was so majestically *there*. Such splendid isolation had cried out to be conquered...

'You looked like one to me—a big, gangly girl, slow as a wet week, with a surly black adolescent glower and a habit of looking down your nose at me as if I were a lower form of life. No wonder I didn't want to have you foisted upon me!'

She immediately felt thick and ungainly, all elbows and knees, the way she used to feel as an wildly overgrown teenager. It was a long time since anyone had made her so clumsily self-aware and she didn't like it. Not at all. Unknowingly she gave him the same filthy black look that she had given him back then.

'When you're my size you can't flit about like a humming bird,' she gritted. 'If I move carefully it's because I have to calculate clearances that other women take for granted. I doubt if you'd want me blundering about among all these antiques. I'm not, and have *never* been, *slow*. Speed is not necessarily an indication of efficiency, you know. In time-and-motion terms, my way is a lot more energy-efficient than if I was rushing about creating a lot of hustle and bustle over tasks that can be performed simply and without fuss!'

If he recognised his favourite phrase being lobbed back in his face, he didn't acknowledge it. Instead, her vehement lecture appeared to amuse him. She made a tentative move around him and he shifted his weight, blocking her path with the mere threat of further movement.

'Mm, so I very quickly discovered. Why do you think I didn't persist in my efforts to get rid of you? You don't appear to exert yourself unduly and yet the work is always done and this house always runs like a well-oiled machine...' If only he had seen her flying up the stairs that morning. Talk about exerting herself unduly! 'If you had been other than supremely capable I'd never have left the supervision of the restorations in your hands. You've never violated that trust. I wasn't criticising you just now, I was simply telling you what my first impressions of you were.'

'Thank you, but I could have done without knowing,' said Vanessa acidly, thinking that his trust would be summarily withdrawn if he knew the truth about her...not merely about last night but the whole ugly mess that had prompted the judge's job offer and her ignominious flight from England.

She wondered what his reaction would be if she blurted it all out now. He would probably run the full gauntlet: shock, horror, distaste. She had seen it all before, from people far less fastidious than Benedict Savage, people who were supposed to have been her friends.

'I thought it time to get it out in the open—so that I might begin to feel less like an interloper here.'

'Interloper?' Vanessa's impatience got the better of her. 'Don't be ridiculous,' she told her employer. 'The house *belongs* to you; you can't be an interloper in your own home.'

A grim smile twitched his hard cheek. 'Can't you?' His voice lifted from a barely audible irony to that familiar ironic crispness. 'But then, this isn't really my home, is it? If one counts a home as a family dwelling, or a residence one has a sentimental attachment to through regular use, I suppose you could call me effectively homeless. I don't think I've spent more than a month at a time at the same address in the last five years.'

The faintly wistful self-derision in his words gave Vanessa a pang but she caught herself before she started feeling too sorry for him. The man was a millionaire for goodness' sake; he had everything he could possibly want and he had the nerve to complain because his life wasn't perfect! There were people in the world—in this country—who lived in cardboard cartons, or worse, and here he was complaining about having too many homes!

'How absolutely frightful for you,' she replied with a crispness that brought his head up with a jerk. 'Jobless *and* homeless. No wonder you're depressed. If I were you I'd be suicidal.'

'If you were me you wouldn't be having the problems I'm having,' he said cryptically, after a tiny pause and an all-encompassing look that made her extremely nervous. 'And I can't envisage you ever taking the easy way out of your problems. You're the type to go down with all guns blazing.'

'I don't approve of firearms,' she said primly, disturbed by the accuracy of his reading of her character.

'We have something in common, then ... other than sharing possession of this house. That is what we do, isn't it, legal ownership not withstanding? You're the one who really makes a home of this house; you're the one who brings it to daily life, who imprints it with personality...'

Vanessa was aghast at the thought that her possessiveness about the house might be the object of amused speculation to others. It was her secret, her little piece of foolish whimsy. Her eyes were stony as she denied her weakness. 'I enjoy seeing the house restored to some of its former glory but I'm the caretaker, that's all. I'm just carrying out your orders.'

'Since I'm hardly ever here to issue them that statement is highly debatable.'

Her eagerness to preserve the state of armed neutrality between them that had made it so easy to treat him as a cypher instead of a human being made her quick to sense criticism.

'If you're not satisfied with my work——'

'I never said that. On the contrary, I'm delighted with the high standards you've maintained in trying circumstances. The restorations are turning out even better than I envisaged. After you've finished your bed-making I'll get you to give me a tour to show me the progress...'

Although bringing him up to date with the work carried out in his absence was a familiar duty that she usually tackled with quiet pride, the thought of spending more time alone in his company while her nerves were still in such a jittery state made Vanessa quail. Fortunately she had a ready excuse at hand.

'I've arranged for some members of the historical society to visit this morning. You did say you didn't mind them being shown around in return for access to their records about the house. Perhaps they could tag along?'

He looked unenthused at the prospect. 'Is Miss Fisher one of them?'

'As a matter of fact, yes,' Vanessa said innocently. The elderly lady, an archetypal twittering spinster, had taken a shine to the elusive new owner of Whitefield and would make a thorough nuisance of herself if she knew he was back in residence.

'In that case I think I might take the Duesenberg out for a couple of hours,' he said hastily. 'You can give me the tour after lunch. If that fits in with your plans, of course.'

'Of course, sir,' she murmured dutifully, heaving an inward sigh of relief as she retreated into the safety of her usual, self-effacing role.

'And don't tell her I'm here,' he scowled.

'Of course not, sir.'

'The woman is a human limpet.'

'Indeed, sir.'

He gave her bland expression a coruscating glare. 'Are you mocking me, Flynn?'

'No, sir,' she lied smoothly.

'Good. Because I can tolerate a lot of things from my employees—insubordination included, if they're good at what they do—but I don't like being laughed at.'

It was definitely an order.

'Nobody does, sir,' Vanessa murmured judiciously. She had noticed that about him—his lack of laughter—it was what contributed to her impression of him as having a somewhat colourless personality. Although he was good-humoured to a fault, he rarely showed any spontaneity. His smile was more of a cynical twist than an expression of warmth. Little seemed to take him by surprise.

Except this morning. This morning he had been caught very much by surprise. The result had been a very distinct loss of that apparently inhuman self-control, and she wondered how much control he had lost last night, when the surprise must have been infinitely greater! She swallowed, her arms tightening possessively on the sheets that bore witness to her own self-betrayal, struggling against the return of her earlier panic. Surely her guilt was stamped all over her face?

Apparently not, because her employer was turning away from her, running his hand rapidly over his chin, the same boyish eagerness in his expression that she had glimpsed in the library, and she realised that his thoughts were running ahead to the birthday present he had been side-tracked from enjoying.

'I don't suppose your historians will be here for a few minutes so it's safe for me to have a shave before I leave. I think I'll take a run up the coast to Coromandel, or maybe even Colville or Port Jackson, if I feel like it. Tell Mrs Riley I'll be back for lunch about one—if you're sure they'll be gone by then.'

'I'll make certain they are, sir,' she assured him. By one o'clock she was sure she'd also be able to persuade herself into a more rational frame of mind.

'Good.' He turned at the entrance to his bathroom, to throw her one more terrifying curve over his shoulder. 'Oh, by the way—don't lock me out again.'

She froze on the threshold of escape. 'I beg your pardon?'

'Downstairs just now. The French doors to the library—you locked them after I went out to look at the car. I had to go around to the front door and knock until Mrs Riley let me back in.'

Vanessa sent up a prayer of thanks. 'Did I? I must have done it automatically. I'm sorry for the inconvenience, sir. It won't happen again.'

Not if she could help it, anyway. The circumstances leading up to her action were, after all, extremely unlikely to recur!

CHAPTER FOUR

'WELL, that should be the last of your rising-damp problem,' Bill Jessop told Vanessa with deep satisfaction as he rose from his crouch in front of the strip of exposed stonework a metre high that ran along the interior wall of what had been the servants' dining-room. 'That last section has dried out nicely. You can get the plasterer to work on it as soon as you like.'

Vanessa followed suit, dusting off her hands as she straightened. 'I just hope we don't find any anywhere else,' she sighed.

'You can't really complain when the place is over a hundred years old,' said the stonemason. 'I think the big problem was that the original builder didn't finish the job. Now *he* was a real craftsman.'

'A pity he succumbed to the gold fever,' said Vanessa with the fine disdain of someone who had never lusted after great riches. 'Instead of drowning in a flooded mine he could have had a long life of quiet prosperity if he'd stuck to his original plan.'

'Maybe it was excitement he was after, rather than the actual gold,' said Bill, a big, stolid man who looked as rough as the materials he worked with. 'Or maybe he was running away from something, or someone. Didn't you say that his wife worked as a cook here for a couple of years after he took off, and had a reputation for being a right old harridan?'

'I don't blame her for being shrewish if her husband deserted her,' said Vanessa tartly. 'Colonial life could be pretty brutal for a woman who didn't have a man to protect her. I'm sure she'd rather have had her husband than the gold.'

'Do you think so? I think she would have been more practical than that. "Gold will buy the highest honours; and gold will purchase love."'

Vanessa spun around, automatically smoothing her hands down the sides of her skirt as she watched her employer pick his way around the ladders and planks that cluttered the doorway.

He had come back from his drive obviously relaxed, his face glowing with wind-burn and his normally economical movements expansive under the lingering effects of high-speed adrenalin. He had described the performance of the powerful car at what Vanessa thought was tiresome length as she'd served his soup, then promptly buried his nose in an architectural magazine while he ate, not even acknowledging the substitution of his empty bowl with a salad, followed by a plate of cheese and crackers. Vanessa had waited until he left the dining-room to take a business call before she'd slipped in to clear the table, congratulating herself that he had appeared to have forgotten his demand for an immediate tour. An oblivious, inattentive and introspective Benedict she was well used to and could handle with ease.

A trickle of dismay slithered down her spine as she realised that she had instinctively referred to him by his Christian name. How had that solecism crept into her thoughts? She glared at him, mentally trying to cram him back into the insulated box labelled 'Mr Savage'. He was not co-operative.

'That's a cynical point of view, Mr Savage,' Bill Jessop said with a conspiratorial male grin. 'I don't think Vanessa is going to agree with you on that.'

She refused to be goaded, folding her hands primly and maintaining a respectful silence as Benedict came to a halt beside them. He had changed, she noticed, into a long-sleeved white polo-shirt which was more casual than anything else she had seen him wear. It must be new, she decided. Something he had brought with him, for she hadn't noticed it in his wardrobe before. The soft draping flattered his lean muscularity, and, tucked into black trousers, emphasised the perfect masculine proportioning of wide shoulders and slim hips.

He looked at her and when she didn't reply his face assumed a bland expression to reflect her own.

'Not me... I was merely quoting Ovid on the Art of Love. That particular piece of cynicism is nearly two thousand years old, but I think that the passage of time has proved the wisdom of his words, wouldn't you say, Flynn?'

She could hardly ignore a direct question but neither did she want to stroke his ego by agreeing with him. 'Then how is it that you're not knighted and married by now?' she prevaricated sweetly, and he laughed.

Vanessa stared. The most humour she had seen him display was a quiet chuckle. His narrow face with its hard, slashing cheekbones, straight, precisely even black brows and high forehead had seemed rigid and austere, the face of a born ascetic. Now, with a sting of shock, she glimpsed a teasing hint of mischief in the warm animation of previously inflexible features, a promise of passion in the relaxed curve of his mouth. In laughter, as in sleep, there was a fullness in his lower lip that was normally disguised by the controlled tautness of his conscious expression. For the first time Vanessa wondered at the origin of that formidable self-control and the faint air of tension that he wore like a cloak—or a suit of armour.

Horrified to find herself studying his mouth with feminine curiosity, Vanessa tore her eyes away, to find that he had stopped laughing and was watching her with an unsettling intentness.

'Perhaps I'm too much of a miser,' he murmured, 'to pay for what I see other men getting for free.'

Bill Jessop laughed at that. 'Nobody who's seen the kind of money you're pouring into this place would call you miserly!'

'Mr Savage looks on it as an investment,' Vanessa pointed out evenly. 'He expects to make a good return on his money by selling as soon as the restorations are finished.' Perhaps it was her very lack of tone that tipped him off, for he was quick to respond, to sense an underlying hostility.

'You think I should be doing it for purely sentimental reasons?' he said. 'Why should I be so altruistic? I have no more historical or personal connection with Whitefield than—than you do.' She stiffened at this casual reminder of her place. 'What would you have me do? Live here permanently myself? The place is far too big for one person, and besides, it's being renovated as an inn. Can you imagine me as a hotelier?'

'Actually, yes,' Vanessa said, stretching her imagination stubbornly. 'You're used to playing host to numerous guests at a time. The only difference is that they would be paying you for the privilege instead of free-loading...' She bit her lip as her true opinion of some of his non-business guests slipped out, but he merely quirked her an oddly considering smile.

'"Playing" being the operative word. I learned a long time ago the value of preventative socialisation as a method of preserving my privacy. A large part of my youth comprised politely displaying for guests. My parents always seemed to be entertaining a continuous flow of friends and new acquaintances. Unfortunately I had no brothers and sisters to take the spotlight off me, so I acquired a fine repertoire of conversational tricks to conceal my shyness and resentment of the instant intimacy that people seemed to think was the required response. I was a Savage and therefore expected to thrive on all the attention. My parents would have been very disappointed in me if they had known how much I hated having to prove myself their son over and over again...'

Vanessa was unnerved by the nonchalance with which he delivered his startlingly frank disclosure. She took an automatic step back, trying to widen the distance between them, but she took with her the mental picture of a quiet, solitary child forced to adopt an adult gregariousness in order to please his parents.

She, too, was an only child but her parents had always made her feel all the more special for being different from them, an individual in her own right. Secure in the circle of their love, she had felt free to rebel and to assert herself, to strike out and make her own mistakes, knowing that any disappointment they felt would be *for* her, not with her.

'It doesn't show,' she murmured.

'I hope that was a compliment, not a comment,' he said smoothly and she realised that he was playing with phrases from their conversation in his bedroom that morning.

'You could always put in a manager and reap the benefits of ownership without the day-to-day hassles,' she said, refusing to acknowledge the significance of his word-play. 'You present the right kind of image: charming yet aloof.'

'Why do I get the feeling that's definitely *not* a compliment?' he murmured back, not giving her time to reply. 'Do I really come across as distant and supercilious? I've always thought of myself as elusive rather than aloof.'

His gaze was engagingly rueful as it met hers, as if he was aware of the inherent romanticism of his self-perception, and was faintly embarrassed by it.

'You can certainly be very elusive when you choose to be,' Vanessa conceded wryly, remembering the numerous times she had had to drag him out for meals. Times when he had shut himself up in his studio with his architectural computer and drawing instruments and left his guests to their own devices.

'No more than you. We had agreed that you were going to bring me up to date on the restorations this afternoon.'

'I was waiting for you to let me know when you were ready,' Vanessa fibbed, conscious of Bill Jessop standing patiently by, his grey eyes bright with interest.

'Really? Is that why I spent ages yanking those damned bell-ropes to no avail?'

Vanessa pinkened at the pleasantly accusing tone. 'I'm sorry, I meant to warn you that the bells have been disconnected while some of the tubing is being replaced.' The vintage mechanical system of zinc tubes encasing sliding copper wires still worked remarkably well and only one or two of the row of bells which hung in the butler's pantry next to the kitchen had had to be replaced.

'Mm, you obviously didn't hear me yelling up and down the halls, either.'

Vanessa raised her eyebrows at him, knowing full well that he had done no such thing. He was too well-trained to stoop to such vulgarity.

'Obviously not.'

'I was beginning to feel like a wraith of my former self... drifting around an empty house with no one to acknowledge my wailing and gnashing of teeth,' he exaggerated lazily. 'I half expected to meet up with my golden-haired ghost again.'

'Ghost?' The stonemason's ears pricked up. 'You've seen a ghost?'

'I told him about Meg,' Vanessa cut in hurriedly, moving determinedly away from the two men in an attempt to draw them apart. 'We won't hold you up from your work any longer, Bill. Mr Savage—shall we start the tour in the drawing-room? It's been papered since you were last here...'

'I certainly saw something in my room late last night,' Benedict said, ignoring her desperate shepherding motion. 'If it was a ghost then she was uncannily lifelike, whoever she was. Have you ever seen this Meg?'

'Well, not myself, no,' Bill replied rubbing his stone-roughened hands together as if to remove a chill. 'But then, I've never been here alone after dark. I've heard tell of some strange goings-on here over the years. Nobody had lived in the place for a couple of years before the judge bought it and it was getting pretty derelict. Personally, I don't know if I believe in ghosts, as such...'

'Neither did I until last night,' said Benedict Savage drily. 'In fact I could have sworn she was as real as you or I.'

'Oh, it always pays to keep an open mind about such things,' Vanessa said quickly. 'The existence of certain psychic phenomena has been well-documented. And if any place can claim to be the site of spiritual turmoil, then Whitefield can. Meg's wasn't the only death by violence here over the last hundred years.'

'You mean I may find myself visited by more apparitions?' He sounded dismayingly intrigued by the prospect. 'How lucky I'm not of a nervous disposition. Perhaps the *Architectural Journal* might be interested in a paper on the subject—the influence of the fifth dimension on architectural conservation. If all my ghosts are as beauteous and willing as the golden-haired Meg I should have no trouble in arousing interest...'

From the corner of her eye Vanessa saw Bill open his mouth to inform him that Meg had been a flaming redhead, not a blonde.

'Yes, I'm sure the historical society would be *very* interested,' she interposed brightly. Willing? What precisely did he mean by *willing*? 'Miss Fisher in particular is a bit of a psychic buff. If she got to hear that you'd had a visitation from the other side, she'd be up here in a flash with her tape-recorder and psychic investigator's handbook, haunting the place herself.'

To her satisfaction her employer blanched, but then he slanted her a keen look. 'For a warning, that sounded distressingly close to a threat, Flynn.'

'I'm sorry, sir,' she murmured with just the correct touch of haughty surprise. 'You told me this morning that you wanted to avoid Miss Fisher and I just thought I should point out the possibility. You know how people in these small communities talk...'

'People might, but since I know you're an utterly loyal and devoted employee, and since Bill here doesn't want to get fired, I don't see how any of this conversation is in danger of leaking out.'

Instead of being offended, Bill laughed. 'I suppose I'd better get back to washing off down that south wall before you decide to fire me, anyway. Nice to see you back again, Mr Savage.' He touched his forelock in a mock-salute as he backed towards the door. 'See you later, Vanessa.'

'Pleasant man,' Benedict Savage commented, running his hand over the mortar in the joints between the grey stone blocks. 'Does a fine job, too. Robert did well to find him.'

Robert Taylor, a specialist restoration architect who worked in the Auckland office of Dane Benedict, had drawn up the plans and a schedule of work for the inn and had been heavily involved in the initial stages...until both he and his boss had realised that Vanessa was more than capable of supervising the ongoing work, even to the extent of employing tradesman as they were required. Now Robert only made a special trip down to Thames as certain, agreed-upon stages were completed.

'Actually, I was the one who found Bill,' said Vanessa quietly. She got on very well with Robert, but he was ambitious and somewhat opportunistic in his eagerness to create a good impression and she thought it did him no favours to let him get away with it too often. 'I'd heard of him through the historical society and seen some of the work he's done in Waihi.'

'I stand corrected.' His casual nod told her that he was aware of his young colleague's failing as he continued, placing a mocking hand over his heart, 'Please, just don't tell me that the ubiquitous Miss Fisher had anything to do with it.'

She couldn't help a small smile escaping the stiffness of her control, her brown eyes lightening with the fugitive gleam.

'No. Madeline's area of expertise is kitchen utensils and cooking-ovens.'

'And ghosts.'

Vanessa's eyes slid away. 'And ghosts,' she conceded reluctantly, feeling herself sinking deeper and deeper in the mire of the foolish deception that had grown out of her choice of diversion. She cleared her throat. 'Where would you like to start your tour?'

'Weren't you anxious to show me the drawing-room a few minutes ago? I was rather distracted last time I was here—I had that Japanese consortium in tow—so I think perhaps you should just show me everything you've done in the last six months. I'm entirely in your hands this afternoon.'

Vanessa looked down at the hands in question. She thought them too large, like the rest of her, but the long, ringless fingers were slender and well-shaped, the round nails short and burnished with natural polish.

He had been in her hands this morning, too, she remembered treacherously. Her palm had been cupped over the rippling tautness of his back, while her left hand had been tucked cosily between their bodies, her fingers curled against his smooth upper chest, measuring the rise and fall of his contented sleep and tingling with the

faint vibration of his steady heartbeat. But of course
that had been nothing to where *his* hands had been . . .

'Flynn?'

Her head jerked up and she felt her skin begin to heat
up as he regarded her with polite puzzlement.

'Er . . . yes . . . good idea. In that case, we'll start with
the main dining-room. The marble mantelpiece came
back from the workshop last week and you'll be able to
see what a difference a professional cleaning job is going
to make on that awful one in the drawing-room . . .'

She was so anxious to escape the intimacy of her
thoughts that she rattled on, inundating him with tech-
nical details as she took him through the public rooms
that were now almost completely restored, albeit with
some discreet modern touches necessary for the comfort
and healthy well-being of future guests, to what they
had been in the former glory years of gold-inspired
prosperity.

Judge Seaton had had the enthusiasm and the knowledge but not the financial resources to indulge in more
than cosmetic improvements to the old building and
Vanessa knew that he would have heartily approved of
the changes that his unknown heir had wrought to what
had been a sorely neglected piece of local history,
whatever Benedict's mercenary reasons for doing so.
Perhaps what had happened had been exactly what he
had been hoping for when he had written that extra-
ordinary codicil to his will. He had known that Vanessa
shared his love of the dilapidated old place, that she
looked upon Whitefield as the home she had never really
had. He had enjoyed inspiring her with his love of history
and perhaps he had been relying on the possessive sense
of belonging he had engendered in her to ensure that
she would maintain a careful watching brief over
Whitefield after he was gone. The thought pleased her
far more than did the notion that he might have made

that stipulation purely out of pity, or concern that she wasn't strong enough to stand on her own two feet.

Her obvious pride of accomplishment didn't escape the man at her side as he meekly allowed himself to be lectured from room to room like a laggardly schoolboy. At first largely silent, he began interrupting her flow with a pertinent question here and there, just enough to encourage her subtly out of the formal recitation of dry facts into expressing a revealing enthusiasm for her subject. When she forgot herself she even moved differently, her stride long and eager, her hips and arms swinging in an uninhibited rhythm, her head and hands contributing expressively to the conversation.

'I'm glad you don't feel that a contemporary bathroom is an unforgivable betrayal of the integrity of the restoration,' Benedict murmured as he surveyed the chaos of plumbing that sprouted from the tiled wall in one of the small upstairs sitting-rooms which were being converted into bathrooms for the adjoining bedrooms.

'This is going to be a working hotel, not a museum,' Vanessa was quick to defend. 'People expect a reasonable standard of accommodation for their money. Tourists may enjoy visiting museums but they don't want to *stay* in them, especially if it means sacrificing their creature comforts. For the sake of strict authenticity we'd have to offer them a wash-stand and chamberpot or portable commode and I don't see many of them wanting to put up with that! The 1870s were still pretty primitive in this part of the world... I mean, the country had only been settled for a few decades and most of the people's energy was going into scraping a living from the land. As long as the public rooms are restored in their period I don't see a conflict, since the kitchens and bathrooms have to be upgraded to meet modern health standards anyway.'

'Mm, hip-baths in front of the fire do rather lose their rustic appeal when you know you have to haul twenty buckets of hot water up the stairs first,' said Benedict musingly.

'*You* wouldn't be doing any hauling,' Vanessa pointed out sourly. 'Except perhaps on the bell-rope.'

'You don't think much of me, do you, Flynn?' he startled her by saying. 'You seem to think I'm incapable of doing anything for myself. A complete wimp, in fact.'

'Of. . . of course not, sir,' she denied, not deceived by his mildness. No man who was a complete wimp could have a body that felt like tensile steel wrapped in warm silk, or dominate, as he did, with a mere look. 'I—it's part of my job to make sure you don't have to do manual labour around the house——'

'During holiday breaks when I was studying architecture, I worked as a building labourer—much to my parents' disgust. I may give the impression that I'm a pampered rich brat but I do make some effort to keep in touch with the real world.'

'Of course you do, sir.'

Her soothing tone made his eyes narrow. 'Are you going to "sir" me to death again now?'

'No, s——' She cleared her throat. She hadn't realised how automatically the word sprang to her lips when she was feeling defensive. 'No, of course not.'

'I hate it when you do that.'

'Do what, s——? Do what?'

'Agree with me in that unspeakably pleasant voice,' he said succinctly. 'And don't say that's what I pay you for. I never did have much respect for yes-men. Or yes-women.'

It was unfortunate that he tagged on that last phrase. It had connotations that made her go hot all over. If she had said yes to him last night she had forfeited a lot more than mere respect!

She stiffened at the dawning gleam of predatory amusement in his gaze as her slight flush made him aware of the sexual overtones of his throw-away remark.

'Although, I'll have to admit, there are certain situations where I love to hear nothing from a woman's mouth *but* the word yes...' he added limpidly, for the sheer pleasure of provoking her.

Her tanned cheeks acquired a deeper, carmine tint and her eyes darkened until they looked like smouldering black coals surrounded by a thick fire-screen of gold-tipped lashes. Her first instinct was to flare back at him, but she resisted fiercely.

'I'm sure there are——' She bit off the sentence before it reached its natural conclusion, but the contemptuous 'sir' hovered unspoken in the air between them and it goaded him further.

'You're blushing, Flynn.'

'That's because I'm embarrassed for you,' she said defiantly.

'Oh?' He looked justifiably wary. 'And why is that, may I ask?'

'Because taunting an inferior who can't fight back is beneath you,' she said with icy disdain.

He winced, acknowledging the skilful thrust before parrying quietly, 'I agree, except that I don't happen to think of any of the people in my employ as inferiors. They are people who work with me as well as for me, and there's give and take on both sides. Your job title may *appear* to make you subordinate to my will but I think we both know that you have a degree of autonomy here which puts you in a rather unique position of authority. I wouldn't even be surprised if, where Whitefield is concerned, you actually consider me *your* inferior...'

Vanessa's eyes flickered guiltily and his expression eased. 'As for fighting back,' he continued, giving her a look of wry respect, 'I think you've just proved that you're more than capable of doing that. I'm duly chastened by your polite disdain for my needling.' He moved restlessly over to the small window which overlooked the kitchen garden and low-walled brick courtyard behind the stables. 'Unfortunately I can't promise I'll never do it again. My moods have been rather unpredictable lately. Maybe I'm going though an early mid-life crisis.'

He sounded irritated with himself and Vanessa was so amused by his unlikely depression that she dared to say, 'I found an old walking stick in the attic last week, Mr Savage; perhaps you'd like me to fetch it for you?'

He spun around. 'Now who's being provoking?' But he was smiling the small, cool smile that was his trademark. 'I suppose you still approach each birthday with joyous anticipation. Wait until you hit thirty, then your perspective will change. I'm amazed that someone so young should have such a preoccupation with history.'

'It's an interest, not a preoccupation, and I'm not so many years younger than you——'

'A decade.' Again he exhibited his phenomenal memory for detail. 'You should still be looking dewy-eyed to the future, not back over your shoulder at the cobwebbed past.'

'We can learn a lot about our options for the future from the evidence of the past,' said Vanessa piously. 'I'm not the youngest in the historical society by a long chalk; we even have primary-school children as members.' She paused, then was unable to resist saying tartly, 'And I was never dewy-eyed.'

'Yes, you were,' he said unexpectedly, studying her wide eyes and grave mouth with its hint of repressed emotion. 'I bet you were brimming with painful innocence until adolescence hit you with a wallop. You must have had more difficulty adjusting than most girls. I suppose you were teased about your size by girls and boys alike, and treated as more mature than you actually were by the world in general.'

Now it was his turn to be amused as she backed off, startled by the thumbnail description of her awkward puberty. 'Don't look at me like that, Flynn; it's not sorcery, it's called applied intelligence. I can make an educated guess because I was teased for exactly the opposite reason. I was a late bloomer, both physically and intellectually. I was nearly seventeen when my voice broke, a string-bean with hardly a muscle to my name at an élite boarding-school where physical evidence of masculinity was the main criterion for judging peer status. To add to my misery I had an astigmatism that means I couldn't wear contact lenses. I passed most of my high-school years as a four-eyed wimp. On the other hand being slight did force me to learn the valuable art of talking my way out of trouble, which in the long run is a far more useful life-skill than the ability to thump the life out of someone smaller than you, don't you think?'

As Vanessa remained silent, stunned by yet another startling new facet of her employer's complex personality, he added coaxingly, 'That's your cue, Flynn, to say, Indubitably, sir, in that insufferably stuffy butler voice that you use to squash my pretensions.'

'I wouldn't dream of it,' said Vanessa weakly, wondering why he was opening up with such devastating intimacy to her just now, when it was vitally important to her mental well-being that he remain a convenient cypher, not a living, breathing human being riddled with intriguing weaknesses.

'Oh, well, in that case, shall we soldier on?' He moved to the open doorway and indicated that she should precede him. 'You can tell me more about the original inhabitants of the inn as we go. The extent of your research certainly makes them seem real. Have you ever been tempted to trace your own family tree? The lawyer said that your mother is a New Zealander...'

'She was,' Vanessa was forced to respond reluctantly. 'She died a few years ago.' Just before the storm over Egon St Clair's death had broken over Vanessa's unsuspecting head. It had highlighted her sense of isolation and, not wanting to worry a father already burdened with grief, she had made mistakes that had only added fuel to the ugly rumours that the St Clair family had circulated.

'I'm sorry. Was it an accident or had she been ill?'

'An illness, but it was very sudden.' Uneasy with the continuing thread of intimacy in the conversation, Vanessa distanced herself with a shrug. 'I do have a few great-aunts and uncles and some second cousins around but most of them live down in the South Island, and that's where the family history is. My mother never really kept in touch after she married Dad and went to England.' A fact Vanessa had been extremely glad of when she had first arrived in the country. The last thing she had wanted was to be inundated with family concern and curiosity.

They were coming to the head of the stairs and Vanessa was about to point out the handmade reproductions of the missing balusters when there was the sound of a car tooting in the front driveway.

'Excuse me, I'll just see who that is,' said Vanessa, welcoming the interruption.

'It can't be anyone for me. No one except Dane knows I'm here...and my personal assistant in New York, but she has express orders not to give out the information.' He kept pace with her on the stairs, reaching the front door first and opening it as if he were the butler and she a departing guest.

'Nice vehicle,' he commented as they stood on the stone steps and watched the driver unfold his considerable height from the front seat of a forest-green Range Rover.

'It's Richard.'

'The stud?' murmured Benedict, eyeing the brawny build and handsome features of the man striding across the gravel towards them.

'He *owns* a stud,' Vanessa hissed, pasting on a smile as Richard approached. Richard usually called before dropping in and if he had done so this morning she could have warned him off. As it was he couldn't have chosen a worse time to turn up out of the blue.

To compensate for her guilty thoughts she strove to sound as welcoming as possible and ended up sounding disgustingly coy. 'Hello, Richard. I didn't expect to see you again so soon.'

Before he could reply Benedict Savage smoothly interposed himself into the conversation by holding out his hand. 'Hello. Wells, isn't it? I was just saying I didn't realise anyone knew I was home.'

'Actually, I came to see Van,' said Richard, smiling pleasantly as he shook hands. Even standing on the second step down he almost topped them both, his bulky oatmeal sweater under the well-worn tweed jacket and working jeans tucked into calf-length boots emphasising his powerful frame. 'She gave me the impression last night that you weren't expected back for a while yet.'

Vanessa tensed. It wasn't beyond the realms of possibility for Benedict, in his present self-confessed state of unpredictable moodiness, to make some crass joke about the cat being away.

To her relief, 'I'm beginning to recognise a certain charm about the place,' was all he said. 'Would you like to come in? We've been looking over the house and were just about to break for coffee.'

That was news to Vanessa, since she would have been the one serving it. He also gave their activities a companionable sound that they had definitely lacked.

'No, thanks.' Richard shook his blond head. 'I just called to drop something off to Van.' He produced the 'something' from his jacket pocket—the tiny vial of perfume that she had filled from the fragile main bottle in her bedroom so that she could carry it in her evening bag. 'It must have dropped on to the floor of my car when you got your keys out.'

Vanessa was hard put to it not to snatch it out of his hand. All it would probably take would be one whiff and Benedict Savage, with his wretchedly superb memory, would connect it instantly with his fragrant ghost!

'Thank you, Richard,' she said, taking it gingerly in her long fingers and tucking it securely in the buttoned breast pocket of her blouse. 'But you needn't have made a special trip.'

'I didn't,' he said in his usual prosaic manner. 'I'm on my way to the vet's and had to go past your gate anyway, so I thought I may as well stop.' His brown eyes crinkled knowingly. 'I also thought it'd give me a chance to check on your health. How's the head this morning?'

Vanessa was aware of Benedict's own head turning her way. 'Fine, thanks,' she said hurriedly.

'Were you feeling ill last night?' Benedict sounded nettled as he studied her profile. 'You could have asked me for the day off. I don't expect you to work until you drop.'

'I was thinking more of her feeling ill *because* of last night.' Richard grinned genially. 'Vanessa had a few too many glasses of champagne.'

'Oh?' Even though she wasn't looking at him she could just *see* the blue eyes sharpen with interest. For the first time Vanessa regretted the qualities that had attracted her to Richard in the first place—his frank openness and the friendly good nature that was incapable of recognising malice. 'Celebrating something, were you?'

'The sale of a stallion of mine . . . and the pleasure of a pretty lady's company, of course,' added Richard gallantly.

'Of course,' repeated Benedict drily and Vanessa swung her head to glare at him. 'I hope you don't mind accepting second-place stakes,' he said blandly, confirming her suspicion that he was laughing at them.

She forgot that she was only interested in curtailing the conversation. 'I'm flattered that Richard wants to share his successes with me. His stud is developing a reputation for producing some of the best thoroughbred horses in Australasia.' There—now let him try to dismiss Richard as an unsophisticated country hick!

'You mean I can expect my butler to come home legless at fairly regular intervals?' was the droll reply.

'I wasn't *legless*,' Vanessa protested coolly, 'I was merely...' She searched for a properly dignified word.

'Over-tired,' Richard interceded diplomatically, then spoiled it by joking, 'Van is a very quiet drunk.'

'No sea-shanties? No brawling? No dancing on the tables?' Benedict smiled engagingly and Richard's good nature fell for it like a ton of bricks.

'I should never have let her polish off most of that second bottle,' he confided, with a grin of masculine fellowship. 'But since I was driving she said it was her moral responsibility to make sure I didn't stray over the alcohol limit. What could I say? Of course, that was before she began to see the funny side of things. I'm afraid I had to hustle her home early when the dreaded giggles struck.'

'You giggle?' Benedict raised a disbelieving eyebrow at her, as well he might. Her face was perfectly stony, rigid with the fear that Richard was going to mention just *how* early he had got her home...

'I think I'm getting that headache you mentioned now, Richard,' she said firmly.

He laughed and accepted the heavy-handed hint. 'And I must get on to the vet's.'

'Are you sure you won't come in? We could have a chat while "Van" finds her aspirin.'

Vanessa gritted her teeth, but fortunately Richard was proof against further charm. 'Some other time. Will you be staying long?'

'I'm not sure. It depends,' Benedict responded with typical reserve, and then took Vanessa's breath away by saying casually, 'I'm considering sectioning off part of the upstairs as a private apartment and putting a manager in to handle the hotel side of things. The finishing work isn't so far advanced that it couldn't accommodate a few more structural alterations without involving too much extra time and money. So I may soon be here more or less permanently, Wells. At my age a man starts to think about settling down...'

When Richard had gone Vanessa asked him sharply, 'What did you say that for?'

'Because I decided that your idea has definite possibilities after all.' And then he neatly curtailed her desire for further discussion on the subject by drawling sarcastically, 'I can quite see the appeal you two might have for each other. You make a magnificently matched pair, negative and positive, fair and dark—an earthy god and a giggling goddess. If you breed true, your children will be a race of thoroughbred Titans! Shall we get on and do the service areas now?'

He turned on his heel and stalked into the house, leaving Vanessa open-mouthed and furious at his insulting audacity.

CHAPTER FIVE

A WEEK later Vanessa was feeling as if she had been flattened by a runaway truck.

She only had herself to blame. She had known her employer would not be able to bear being bored for much longer than a few hours. He might have decided he *needed* a holiday, but he didn't really *want* one.

What he really wanted, she'd realised after days of watching him restlessly poke and pry and question everything she had done or planned to do, was *change*. He was rebelling against the subtle regimentation of his well-ordered professional life and her impulsive suggestion had provided him with the perfect challenge, an opportunity to be whimsical, since she couldn't believe he really intended to give up his peripatetic lifestyle to languish in the backwater of a small-town inn.

Unfortunately, his method of indulging a personal whimsy had proved to be every bit as serious, meticulously planned and competitive as everything else he did. First, he'd decided that he needed to know every detail of Whitefield's history and reconstruction; he had even called Robert Taylor down for a special consultation, and had gone over all Vanessa's old reports with a fine-tooth comb. Then he had started to prowl.

With the Duesenberg only a fond memory—how Vanessa wished that Dane Judson had leased it for a week instead of merely a weekend—there was nothing to lure Benedict away from the house, and everywhere she'd turned he'd seemed to be relentlessly underfoot. After having had virtual free run of Whitefield for most of the last three years it had been extremely disconcerting to have to confer and defer to a higher power and Vanessa had disliked it even more than she had expected that she would.

She couldn't even get on with her routine daily duties in peace because she was constantly being interrupted with requests for information or assistance. It had been a strain trying to maintain the proper barrier of correctness between them when his own reserve had slipped a little further each day, but somehow she'd managed it, even though it meant her patience was worn to a frazzle. For all his apparent willingness to treat her as an equal, she knew from bitter experience that it didn't do to trust the motives of rich young employers, no matter how benevolent they might seem. Better to be safe in discretion than risk the sorry consequences of being caught out of your place.

Kate Riley, who didn't live in and had only relatively brief face-to-face encounters with their employer, had had a much rosier view of the proceedings.

'He's turning out a bit of a surprise, isn't he—not so stuffy as we all thought?' she said approvingly as she buttered scones for his afternoon tea three days after his arrival. He had told her he would prefer plain, hearty country cooking to the more sophisticated menu of New Zealand delicacies he invariably asked Vanessa to draw up for his visitors—another valuable point in his favour. Country born and bred, Kate didn't consider a man a real man unless he ate plenty of meat and potatoes. And butter, she declared, was what had made the country great!

'You know, I think his real trouble was he never learned to enjoy himself,' she continued, adding lashings of her own blackberry jam. 'What good has having all that money done him, I ask you? Rush, rush, rush...no wonder he never had much to say for himself; the poor man's brain must have been in a constant whirl. This is the first time he's come without his secretary at his heels and look at the good it's done him already! He's as happy as a sandboy, pottering about the place. A real chip off the old block.'

Vanessa, who didn't know what a sandboy was but knew that Benedict's fax-modem had been running hot late into the night, every night, thought that was going too far.

'He was only very vaguely related to Judge Seaton, you know. I don't see any similarities between them at all,' she murmured.

'We'll see,' was all Kate replied, investing the time-honoured phrase with its customary smugness.

He certainly shared at least one of the old judge's less endearing traits, Vanessa had to admit later that day, when she found herself barring the way to the small room which led off the butler's pantry.

Stubbornness.

'I would prefer that you didn't,' she said, using the advantage of her height to block him looking over her shoulder, past the door he had managed to whisk open.

'Why? What have you got to hide?' He had wandered into the kitchen for a cold drink and then lingered to inspect the bells which had just been rehung in the pantry, though not reconnected yet. Vanessa had been polishing a canteen of silver, trying so hard to ignore his disruptive presence that she hadn't been quite quick enough when he had spied the discreet panelled door set back into the far pantry wall, overlooked in his previous glance at the pantry and adjoining larder and scullery.

'Nothing,' she said, hanging desperately on to the door-handle and trying to pull it closed behind her. Unfortunately he had moved too close for her to do so without brushing against his body. 'Because there's nothing much to see. All it needs is a floor-sand and a paint job——'

'Then you won't mind me having a look.'

'You never wanted to look before.' She dropped her shoulder as he attempted to duck underneath it.

He straightened and gave her a quizzical smile. In a white shirt and casual, double-breasted navy blazer, one hand thrust into his trouser pocket, he looked lazily relaxed, but there was a distinct threat in his closeness and the steadiness of his gaze. Her awareness of the sinewy strength that lay under his clothes made her doubly nervous.

'I've never been interested before,' he said simply. 'You complained that I wasn't taking a personal enough interest in the inn. Now that I am you seem to resent it. Did you think you could set parameters to my interest? Defend your own hallowed piece of turf when you have free run of mine? Are you refusing to let me see your room, Flynn?'

Vanessa swallowed at the silken enquiry. She had acted purely on instinct and now she was being made to feel thoroughly foolish.

'And what if I did?' she asked, more out of nervousness than defiance.

'I'd respect your right to privacy.'

He lifted a hand at the same moment as he spoke and she flinched at the sudden movement, then flushed when she saw that he was merely removing his glasses.

She had never seen him without them before and she was amazed at the difference it made to his appearance. Like his laughter, his unprotected eyes made his face look immediately softer, less austere. Younger, too, and curiously unguarded, his pupils expanding hugely to draw more light into his myopic gaze, leaving only a thin outer rim of clear blue iris, of such intensity of colour that it was almost luminous. It was also mildly hypnotic and Vanessa leaned forward in fascination.

'Unless, of course, you changed your mind and moved aside,' he murmured softly, and suddenly his hands clamped mercilessly around her waist and he spun gracefully around with her as if she weighed no more than a feather, setting her back down on the freshly polished pantry floorboards. While she was still wondering exactly what had happened, he coolly replaced his glasses and he strolled unimpeded into her room.

'My God, I can see you wouldn't be able to do much entertaining in here,' he said abruptly, openly appalled at the sight of the single box-bed, dressing-table piled with books and the huge, tasteless Victorian free-standing wardrobe that took up most of the floor space in the cramped room. The single small window looked straight out on to the garden wall. 'Two people in here would be a crowd!'

Vanessa was still trying to get control of her breathing. He hadn't even broken a sweat picking her up!

'It's adequate for my needs,' she said unevenly, hovering back at the door.

'Adequate!' he exploded, turning to look at her to see if she was being sarcastic. She wasn't, which seemed to annoy him further. 'What are you, a masochist? Don't tell me it was the judge's idea for you to live in this...monk's cell. By all accounts he allowed you as much licence as you cared to take—as do I for that matter. You know damned well you could have set yourself up in practically any room in the house!'

She shrugged. 'It's convenient, and since I don't spend much time in there anyway——'

'Oh, I see. So now I should feel guilty because you work such long hours that you don't have any time left over to spend in your own quarters——'

She was impatient now. 'That's not what I meant. I have plenty of spare time, I just don't choose to spend it shut up in my bedroom. You said you didn't want the house closed up like a tomb when you weren't here, that the most efficient way to air a room was to make use of it, so that's what I do. When I read or sew or knit I try to use a different room each time——' She broke off as she realised she was stepping on very thin ice. Any moment she was going to tell him about her methods of similarly airing the beds in sixteen bedrooms, including his . . .

'What very domesticated hobbies you have, Flynn,' he drawled and she frowned, wondering whether he was insulting her or merely making an innocent comment. There was a small gleam in his eye that made her wish he hadn't put his glasses back on. They were too effective a screen for his emotions.

'Given your insistence of job equality between the sexes I would have thought your interests would have a more feminist bias. At least now I know why I almost spiked myself on a knitting-needle on the drawing-room sofa the morning after I arrived. And I ran across several copies of *Vogue* and *Metro* tucked among the *Architectural Digests* in the library.'

'I was only obeying your instructions about the house,' she said stiffly. 'I always tidy my things away before you come——'

'And thereby leaving the rooms looking as sterile and unlived-in as a *Digest* photographic layout,' he murmured.

'I thought that was what you wanted, Mr Savage——'

'You mean you assumed it was.'

'You never bothered to correct my assumptions,' Vanessa pointed out coldly.

'Probably because I didn't realise myself how wrong they were,' he said, half under his breath. Before she could think how to respond to that cryptic remark he had turned back to view the room critically. 'We definitely have to do something about this room.'

'I told you, it's perfectly adequate——' Vanessa began, thinking that he was introducing radical changes in her life at an ever-increasing rate. Why couldn't he let her get used to one change before initiating the next? Or let her have it all at once, so that at least it would be over and done with.

'Adequate in Victorian times perhaps, but hardly these days. Not everyone has your evident taste for spartanism, Flynn. Don't you find it claustrophobic trying to sleep in here?'

It was unfortunate that at that very moment Kate Riley had come into the pantry to collect a casserole dish and she paused behind Vanessa just long enough to chuckle, and say, 'I tell her that myself, Mr Savage, her being such a big girl and all, but Van says she's a very compact sleeper. Mind you, she doesn't sleep in her own bed too often these days—if she had to cram herself into that little bed every single night of the year I'm sure it'd be a different story!'

She bustled away, still chuckling, and for the second time in a few days Vanessa was privileged to see her employer shocked speechless.

For a moment she thought the jig was up and she flushed miserably as his eyes swept incredulously over her from the tip of her practical shoes to the paranoically tamed hair on the top of her head, no doubt mentally stripping and vainly trying to superimpose her over the explicit image inside his head. Then she was the one speechless as he said icily, 'And I thought you lived a cloistered, unexciting life here, far from the madding crowd. Another example of the dangers of assumption. That prim-and-proper air of yours is obviously misleading. You must have quite a reputation if even Mrs Riley accepts your sexual antics—or should I say athletics?—as merely routine.' His expression was very much the ascetic as he continued harshly, 'However, I'm not inclined to be so generous. When I said you were welcome to have friends come here I wasn't issuing you a licence for promiscuity——'

'I am *not* promiscuous——' began Vanessa, with tight-lipped precision. There was something richly ironic in being thought promiscuous because of her fervent attempts *not* to appear promiscuous. And she was innocent on both counts!

'Good. So it's only Wells' bed that you forsake your own for, is it?' he interrupted, adding dangerously, 'At least, I *hope* you go to his place for your little romps, because, when you're here under *my* roof, as far as I'm concerned you're on duty and I'm not paying my caretaker to have sex——'

'Richard and I do not "have sex,"' she hissed furiously, side-tracked by the outrageous crudity of his insult.

'Sorry, *make love*,' he corrected himself sarcastically.

'How dare you——?'

'Prim and proper won't wash any more, Flynn. I dare because I pay the bills here and therefore I get to set the rules of conduct. While you live under my roof I'm responsible for your health and well-being, and I've always taken my responsibilities seriously.' He gave her another narrow-eyed look.

'No wonder you're so tense and jittery lately. My being here is obviously hampering your freedom—you're not getting your usual quota of...*lovemaking*.' He stressed the words with mocking deliberation. 'Well, just be patient. I'm off up to Auckland at the end of this week, to an Institute of Architects awards presentation. I'll stay in the apartment overnight so you'll be able to entertain your lover at leisure. Just remember the rules. I don't care what you do under his roof, but under mine you're as celibate as a nun!'

Vanessa had longed to throw his hypocrisy in his face but the impulse died as swiftly as it was born. Why give him even more powerful ammunition for his pot-shots? Trust him to confuse friendship and genuine human warmth with crude physical desire, she simmered as she watched him leave, wishing she had the courage to heave the canteen of cutlery at the back of his supercilious head. It would give new meaning to the term knifed in the back. She would enjoy seeing him forked and spooned as well!

It obviously hadn't even occurred to him that she might be *in love* with Richard, might be a misty-eyed romantic whose dreams he had just callously trampled into the mire. No, he thought only in clinical terms of lust and appeasing an appetite. No wonder he had never married. He probably wouldn't recognise love if it hit him in the face.

And, to show that his opinions about her personal life were totally irrelevant, she was ruthlessly good-mannered to him for the rest of the week, which sadly had the opposite effect to that which she had intended. Instead of losing interest under the avalanche of politeness he seemed to delight in testing the limits of her patience, tossing personal comments into seemingly innocent conversations like miniature grenades that threatened to blow apart her armoured reserve.

By Friday Vanessa was clinging on to her composure by the skin of her teeth and it was with unutterable relief and a sneaking sense of victory that she watched him depart for Auckland. For the most part she had successfully held out against his flagrant manipulations. But her resistance had taken its toll. In a week he had cranked up her stress level higher than it had been for years and she welcomed the chance for a respite, however brief, in order to rebuild her shaky defences. Perhaps by the time he came back he would have forgotten his game, or be bored by it, and things could return to a semblance of normality.

When Richard rang soon after the BMW had cruised out of the gates and asked her if she wanted to have dinner with him that evening, Vanessa accepted with alacrity.

A nice, soothing night in Richard's undemanding company was just the antidote she needed to a severe

overdose of Savage teasing. Since they had decided to
eat at a fashionably late hour Vanessa took her time
getting ready, pampering herself as she hadn't done in
a long time, even painting her nails.

As she got dressed in her newest gown—a black crêpe
de Chine streaming out to mid-calf from the fitted,
halter-necked bodice—she determined to devote herself
to showing Richard that she was now ready to progress
from friendly hugs and kisses to something more
meaningful.

She ran a brush through her loose hair and then raked
it back from her forehead and ears with her fingers and
gave it a quick spritz with a firm-hold hairspray to stop
the loose strands from annoying her while she was eating.
Of course, they probably would anyway, but a woman
needed one frivolity in her life and with Vanessa it was
her hair.

She surveyed herself in the age-spotted mirror on the
wall of her room and nodded as she spun around, pleased
with the way the thin crêpe de Chine of the skirt flowed
around her legs. It looked just the way the photo did in
the *Vogue* pattern book. The stiffened bodice, fastened
from waist to collarbone by thirty tiny covered buttons
hooked through satin loops and detailed with top
stitching, had caused her a lot of trouble when she was
making it, but the end result had been worth all her
cursing and unpicking. Her bared shoulders were a little
unseasonal but she knew the restaurant that Richard was
taking her to was small and warm so she merely wrapped
herself in a three-quarter-length black mohair cardigan-
coat for the car trip.

'Looks rather spooky in the moonlight, doesn't it?'
said Richard as they drove away from the inn.

Vanessa looked back at the ragged outline of gables
and chimneys, the slate roof gleaming darkly in the light
of a richly overripe moon. Crouched in a small valley
just off the main Thames coastal-road, with the foothills

of the Coromandel Range rising steeply in the background and no other visible signs of the thriving community which existed just over the hill, the inn did look rather Gothic. The main design of the inn was a long stone T-shape, with the kitchen and service areas jutting out at the back, but the uncompromising sternness of the stone shape was softened by the addition of ornate wooden-covered verandas which ran the length and breadth of both storeys, supported on huge pillars of heart kauri milled from the native forests, for which the area was justly famous. The carriage light at the front door which she had left burning only seemed to emphasise the completeness of the shadowy building's isolation.

'That reminds me, has Savage tracked down his ghost yet?'

Vanessa gave him a sharp look. 'How did you hear about that?'

He grinned. 'Word gets around.'

Vanessa gave an inward groan. She might have known that Bill Jessop wouldn't keep his mouth shut. She wondered whether Richard suspected the source of the hoax, but his handsome features were harmlessly amused as he concentrated on negotiating the narrow, winding road.

'He's been into the newspaper office, Melissa says, going through hundred-year-old files. She said he took away photocopies of reports about Meg's murder.'

'Oh?' Vanessa was distracted from her immediate worry by the realisation that Richard had seen Melissa Riley recently. Had it been a date or just a casual meeting? Since she had insisted she wasn't ready for exclusivity the idea of him seeing other woman had never bothered Vanessa before. To her dismay it didn't really bother her now, either. Surely she ought to feel jealous of the man she intended...

Intended what? That was the problem—she still didn't really know what her intentions towards him were. Richard's intentions towards her she could guess; from the gallantly cautious way he was treating her they were of the most honourable kind. He would be happily willing to take her to bed but she had no doubts that ultimately it was marriage that he wanted from her. He was in his mid-thirties and ready to settle down. Unlike someone else she could name. The trouble was that she had a hard time imagining herself in bed with Richard while she was having much difficulty imagining herself *out* of bed where Benedict Savage was concerned!

The small cottage restaurant was filled to capacity. It had a good reputation for excellent food at reasonable prices and was highly popular with local residents who wanted to dress up and eat somewhere a bit more special than the pub or one of the fast-food restaurants that commonly sprang up at normally sparsely populated, seasonal holiday destinations like the Coromandel.

When Richard accepted the wine-list he looked over at her and grinned. 'Champagne, my dear?'

Vanessa's determination shivered. 'What about red tonight? I think I'm going to have the venison,' she said, pretending not to understand the reference.

'Right. But only one bottle this time, OK?'

Vanessa gave him a mock-glare as the waitress drifted away. 'Now she's going to think I'm a lush.'

'I wouldn't blame her. You do look rather lush this evening.' His eyes dipped to the neckline of her dress which she had left unbuttoned as far as the swell of her breasts to give a more casual look. It also revealed more cleavage than usual and, given the way the light boning of the bodice lifted her breasts, she couldn't blame Richard for taking it as an invitation to look. That was what she had intended, wasn't it?

'Why, thank you, kind sir,' she said flippantly, feeling that she ought to blush at the intensity of his gaze but unable to summon the required rush of excited blood. 'You look rather gorgeous yourself.'

To her amusement he produced the flush that had eluded her, visibly moved by her teasing flattery. She felt a surge of tenderness for him. Dear Richard; she couldn't think of one good reason why she shouldn't fall madly in love with him.

To that end she flirted gently with him through the leisurely meal and was waiting for her dessert, sipping the last of the smooth Australian red wine he had ordered, when she suddenly choked.

'Van, are you all right?'

'Yes.' She coughed, blinking her eyes rapidly to clear them of tears. The vision on the other side of the room blurred, then steadied again. It was a delusion; it had to be! Then the man speaking persuasively to the hostess turned full-face to the room. It was Benedict Savage—supposedly safely ensconced at a posh banquet in Auckland—sinfully overdressed in a white dinner-jacket and black tie. Oh, *God*! Furtively Vanessa looked around. The waitress had removed the lavishly large menus when she had taken their order and there wasn't even so much as a pot-plant to hide behind.

'Van, what's the matter? You look as if you've seen a ghost.'

That wretched word again! Vanessa produced a feeble smile. Thank goodness Richard was sitting opposite across the table instead of on the banquette seat beside her, and had his back to the open foyer. With any luck the hostess would just explain to Benedict that the restaurant was full and send him on his way. The kitchen shut down at eleven, and it was nearly that now, although the restaurant itself didn't close until midnight and people usually made the most of their night out by lingering over special coffees or to dance in the small adjoining room where the chef's wife played the piano. Anyway, no one got in these days without a reservation. But if Richard saw him he was bound to acknowledge him in his usual polite way, perhaps—horror of horrors—even invite him to join them!

'Some wine went down the wrong way,' she explained hurriedly, and with perfect truth.

Just in time she saw the light glint off Benedict's spectacles as he lifted his head to look into the room over the hostess's shoulder and she brushed her dessert fork off the table with her elbow and ducked down to pick it up in one fluid movement.

'Whoops, excuse me!' Her head pressed against the bottom of the table, she pretended to grope for her lost implement, her heart thumping as she congratulated herself on her quick reflexes.

'Don't worry about it, Van; I'll get you another one. You won't be able to use one that's been on the floor, anyway.' Too late Vanessa saw the flaw in her impulsive plan. Richard had already raised his voice to attract the attention of their waitress. 'Excuse me, Kylie, could we have another fork here?'

Half crouched under the table, Vanessa closed her eyes and prayed, deaf to the soft hum of conversation and discreet clatter of crockery and cutlery from the patrons around them. All she could hear were the approaching footsteps that sounded like the knell of doom.

'Thanks. Just leave it, Van. Kylie's brought another one.'

Vanessa's panic eased a moment too soon at his quiet reassurance. She was cautiously beginning to ease upright as she heard Richard suddenly rise and say, 'Hello, Savage. What are you doing here? I thought you were up for some big award in Auckland tonight?'

Vanessa froze, thinking stupidly that she hadn't known Benedict was in line for one of the awards, as she listened to the casual reply. She opened her eyes and saw the polished black shoes planted beside the table leg. Shoes that she herself had buffed to their shellac shine the previous afternoon.

'I was. I decided to come back early.'

'Come straight from there, I suppose?' Richard guessed, obviously looking at the white jacket as he ventured another sympathetic guess. 'Missed out, did you? I don't blame you for ducking out early. Those type of things can certainly drag on if you don't have anything to celebrate. But if you called in here for a nightcap on the way home you made a bit of a mistake; they don't run a separate bar.'

'So I just discovered.' There was an excruciating pause, then he said sardonically, 'I hesitate to sound indelicate, but whatever your companion is doing under the table she seems to be doing very thoroughly. That is, I assume it *is* a woman?'

Richard, the idiot, saw it as a joke rather than the subtle insult that made Vanessa go hot all over. 'If you saw her dress you wouldn't ask that question! Are you running out of air down there yet, honey?' he said, his voice threaded with wicked laughter.

It was all so humiliating, Vanessa thought as she clenched her teeth and slowly unfolded herself, the errant fork clutched in her sweaty palm.

She knew that her face was red and her hair was falling all over her face. She was certain that Benedict knew who she was and was just doing this to embarrass her. Sure enough, when her eyes emerged far enough to peep sullenly over the table-top, she could see an expression of malicious satisfaction on Benedict's face as he glanced at Richard.

For her he had a faintly quizzical smile as she reluctantly sat upright, his eyes sinking to the exposed cleft between her breasts before lifting, lifting as she straightened to her full height. The quizzical amusement faltered as his gaze went over the thick blanket of hair that she quickly tucked back behind her ears.

It vanished entirely when he looked back at her flushed face, *really* looked this time, and she knew that he hadn't realised, not until then. He had thought Richard was dining with some other woman.

'*Flynn*?'

Her smile was a mere twitch. 'Hello, Mr Savage; fancy seeing you here.'

Her attempt at bright surprise fell flat as a lead balloon. He stared at her, his eyes leached from blue to sleet-grey as he leaned back so that he got a better look at the hair rippling down between her shoulder-blades.

A nervous tic suddenly began to pull at the skin on his left temple and Vanessa began a fatalistic countdown to the imminent explosion. She could only hope that his rigorous self-control and distaste for emotional display would rescue her from complete public annihilation!

CHAPTER SIX

IT WAS Richard who unknowingly defused the ticking time bomb.

'Why don't you sit with us and have your drink?' he suggested blithely. 'Van and I are just waiting for our dessert. I'm sure the management won't quibble if they know you're our guest. After all, you don't look as if you'll cause any trouble.'

Little did he know, thought Vanessa as, to her horror, the offer was smoothly accepted.

'Why not? Unless *Van* objects. Do you... *Van*?'

She wished he would stop saying her name like that. It was enough to make her hair curl—if it hadn't been a coiled mass of ringlets already.

'Why should I object?' she squeaked bravely.

'I don't know... guilt, perhaps.'

'Guilt?' Why didn't he sit down if he was going to, instead of looming over her like that? There was a perfectly good empty chair next to Richard. She wasn't going to let him bully her with stand-over tactics. 'I've got nothing to feel guilty about,' she lied brazenly.

'No? How about leaving me to come home to a cold, dark, deserted house?'

His mock-pathos made her heart flip-flop in her chest. Perhaps her fate wasn't so cut and dried after all. Maybe she had mistaken that searing look. Perhaps he was just in a foul mood after losing out on an award he had wanted.

'You weren't supposed to be coming home. But as it happens I left a light on—and the oil-fired heating going.' She adopted a conciliatory tone.

'I notice you don't dispute the deserted bit.' To her dismay he didn't take the chair beside Richard. Instead he slid on to the banquette beside her. She felt the heat of his thigh even though he remained a decorous distance away on the upholstered leather bench. 'Unless, of course, you count my ghostly courtesan. Sorry, Flynn, I mean *actress*... What lovely hair you have, by the way,' he continued in the same mild, conversational tone. 'And what a lot of it.'

'She looks quite different, doesn't she, with that mane flying free?' said Richard affably, relaxed by his good meal, and cheerfully oblivious to the undertones.

'Very different. So different, in fact, I nearly didn't recognise her,' said Benedict, shifting on to his hip so that his body was curved towards hers, still a safe distance away and yet suffocatingly close. Vanessa continued to look towards Richard with a fixed smile, her back stiff, conscious that with the blind end of the banquette on her other side she was very effectively trapped.

'Continuing the equestrian analogy, Wells, what would you call that colour?' he mused lightly. 'Golden palomino?'

'Palominos may have golden coats but their manes are always cream or white. Vanessa's colouring is definitely bay.' Richard chuckled.

'Do you mind? This is a restaurant, not a stable,' Vanessa cut in sharply, perversely as annoyed with Richard as she was with Benedict. 'If you came in here gasping for a drink, shouldn't you order one?'

There was a tiny, splintering silence.

'Oh, are you talking to me? I didn't realise—you weren't looking in my direction,' came the purr by her ear and she was forced to turn her head to meet the challenge of his stare.

Did he or didn't he?

Was he baiting her or was her paranoia colouring his innocent words with perilous meaning? He hadn't seen her face, she reminded herself desperately, so he couldn't be absolutely certain, not on such flimsy evidence as her hair.

'Let me buy that drink for you—it'll be easier all round if I just add it to my bill.' Richard interrupted the wordless duel with his customary generosity. 'What would you like? A whisky?'

At Benedict's careless nod he turned in his seat and beckoned the waitress again.

Benedict hadn't taken his eyes off Vanessa and now his voice lowered for her ears alone. 'Is all that hair as soft as it looks, I wonder?' As he spoke he ran a hand lightly down from the top of her skull to the uneven ends of the thick pelt. Vanessa nearly shot out of her seat. Every nerve-end in her scalp seemed to spit and crackle.

'I'm sorry, did I hurt you?' he murmured, his eyes glittering in the light of the flickering candle in the centre of the small table.

'No,' Vanessa gritted. He can't prove a thing, she repeated to herself in a mental chant. All she had to do was hold him off until they got home. Or, better still, until tomorrow, when he might be in a more receptive frame of mind.

'Mmm, it's even softer than it looks.' He stroked again, this time sinking his fingers into the corkscrew ripples and drawing a swath forward over her shoulder. His knuckles brushed the bare skin of her upper arm, sending a fresh shiver of awareness right down to her toes. 'And very attractive against your black dress and pale skin. Such a surprising colour variation, too; it almost looks *golden* in this candlelight. And so light and *fleecy*, such a *fluffy* confection...'

He leaned towards her as he toyed with the captive locks, his nostrils flaring slightly, and her heart jerked in her breast at each tightening of his lethally soft voice on the trigger words.

'Do you mind?' She reached up to push her hair back out of his grasp, discovering to her embarrassment that she was still holding the fork in a white-knuckled grip.

Resisting the temptation to stab him with it, she shifted instead so that her back was to the corner of the banquette, tossing her head so that her hair fell into the shadow behind her. She laid the fork down on the white tablecloth in front of her and then began to fiddle nervously with it as she tried to think of an innocuous starting point for a polite conversation.

When she finally plucked up the courage to give him a quick, sideways glance it was to find him staring down at her hands with their carefully painted nails. Hoping he hadn't noticed their faint nervous tremor, she clenched her fists, and then froze as his fingertip tracked slowly over the white cloth and up over the ring-finger of her right hand.

'That's an interesting ring you're wearing. Silver and jade, isn't it?'

'Yes, a jeweller at a craft commune up past Coromandel made it,' she babbled eagerly, automatically splaying her hand, as much to shake off his touch as to display the large, ornate ring. Local crafts. You couldn't get much more innocuous than that. 'This area is quite famous for the number of artists and artisans——'

'It's an extremely unusual design. One might even say... unique.'

There was something odd in his voice, a note of repressed exultation, that brought Vanessa up short just as she was about to agree. The ring. She had been wearing the ring that night and hadn't bothered to take it off before she crashed into his bed!

'Oh, I don't know, she probably stamps them out by the dozen for the tourist trade,' she said with a hectic little laugh.

But Richard was there to keep her on the straight and narrow, the directest possible route to her downfall...

'Not at those prices, Van,' he said as he turned back from ordering. 'I was with you when you bought it last spring, remember? You didn't want to part with that much until the woman told you everything she did was strictly one-off.'

'Rather like having a personalised number-plate strapped to your finger,' murmured Benedict maliciously. 'Distinctive and gratifyingly easy to trace.'

Vanessa's nerve broke, her hand lifting in a helpless warding-off gesture. 'Mr Savage, I——'

He caught her hand in an unpleasantly tight grip and returned it to the table. 'Is this your dessert arriving with my drink? It looks delicious.'

Vanessa looked at the sticky chocolate concoction placed before her. What had made her mouth water fifteen minutes ago now made her feel ill.

'What's the matter? Digestion playing up?' Benedict taunted over the top of his whisky glass.

Gotcha! his expression said, and like an automaton Vanessa picked up her spoon, deciding she would eat the damned thing if it killed her. Perhaps it would be better if it did!

The decision was taken out of her hands when Benedict intercepted her first spoonful by guiding it, not to her own mouth but to his.

'Mmm, whisky and chocolate, a heady combination...'

She watched mesmerised when his lips slowly parted and his tongue curled under the bowl of the spoon as he took the spoon into his mouth. Her pulse began to thump against the fingers that had encircled her wrist. There was something disturbingly erotic about the way he fed from her hand. His jaw flexed, cheeks hollowing as he sucked the smooth chocolate mousse from the spoon. He seemed to take an inordinate length of time about it, although it was only a few seconds of real time, and when he released the spoon his tongue ran lightly across his upper lip, collecting the residual sweetness. Helplessly she wondered what his mouth had felt like on hers. Had he licked her as delicately and sensuously as he'd feasted on the chocolate? A tingle shot through her body and her lips parted in unconscious imitation of his actions. Her eyes rose, to be captured by his, a fiercely knowing look in them that made her want to sink through the floor.

She knew she was blushing wildly and she looked hurriedly at Richard but he was content, enjoying his own serving of apple pie, blissfully unaware of the sizzling tension across the table. Oh, *Richard*! She felt a fleeting sense of despair for something slipping irretrievably beyond her grasp.

She looked nervously back at Benedict. His eyes had shifted from grey to blue and for the first time she appreciated the true meaning of the phrase 'looking blue murder'.

He looked as if he could cheerfully throttle her, and yet there was another emotion there that was even more terrifying, a tigerish gleam of primitive masculine triumph that hinted that it wasn't her mere death that he was contemplating.

Oh, God, surely she hadn't made any reckless promises to him in the throes of drunken passion? Surely he couldn't expect to hold her to anything she might have said or done in a state of alcoholic irresponsibility?

'Mr Savage——'

His smile was cruelly brilliant at her breathless plea. 'Oh, call me Ben, please...after all, you're off duty tonight and that makes us equals. Besides, such overt formality is rather silly in the circumstances, isn't it—Vanessa...?'

Somehow he made her name redolent with sin, the 's's sliding slowly off his tongue like lazy serpents and coiling seductively around her throat, making it difficult to breathe, let alone defend herself.

'I——'

'One taste just isn't enough . . . may I have another? I've just discovered an insatiable appetite for your delights.'

He was looking at her mouth and for a moment she misunderstood his husky plea and glared at him in seething outrage.

'The chocolate mousse, Nessie,' he clarified limpidly, guiding her hand with gentle force back to her plate, his forearm brushing the outer curve of her breast as he made her dip and lift the spoon again to his mouth.

She let the handle go and was relieved when he released her without fuss to take hold of it himself.

'You may as well eat the whole thing,' she said, shoving the plate sourly in his direction, realising that his tormenting had only just begun. Well, she might have to take it but she didn't have to like it. If he claimed they were equal then she was going to act it by asserting what little pride she had left. 'And please don't call me by that ridiculous nickname.'

His eyebrows rose, deliberately misunderstanding her. 'Nickname? You mean *Van*? I must admit, it is rather terse and unattractive.'

Richard looked up at the mention, his handsome brow wrinkling with concern as he regarded her irritated expression. 'Don't you like it? But all this time . . . why on earth didn't you say——?'

'No, I meant Nessie—as he knows very well!' Vanessa struggled not to let her resentment at Benedict spill over on to the only innocent party at the table. 'It makes me sound like somebody's old nanny.'

'I was thinking more in terms of the Loch Ness monster,' said Benedict glibly, taking another leisurely swallow of her dessert. 'You know—mysterious, elusive, appearing when you least expect her...'

'Sounds like rotten butler material to me, Savage,' Richard joked.

Benedict looked at him with a pleasant smile that Vanessa instantly distrusted.

'On the contrary, it makes her ideal. ''The noblest service comes from nameless hands, and the best servant does his work unseen''.'

'Ovid again?' Richard showed that his memory was much better tuned than his jealous instincts.

'Oliver Wendell Holmes. I'm sure the quotation must be in all the best butler manuals, isn't it, Vanessa?'

She looked him dead in the eye and smiled crisply. 'Why, yes, right next to the one that says that few men are admired by their servants; ''Many a man has been a wonder to the world, whose wife and butler have seen nothing in him that was in the tiniest bit remarkable''.'

His narrow mouth curved in droll appreciation, as if he knew the extent of dramatic licence she had taken with the quotation. 'I think I'd rather settle for being a wonder to my wife and unremarkable to the world. A much more comfortable affair.'

'''Affair'' being the operative word, since you don't have a wife,' she shot sceptically back. He was already a wonderboy in the architectural world so it was unlikely that any wife he took would have any choice but to accept that most of his passion was devoted to his work.

He inclined his head. 'Not at the moment, no. So that only leaves my servants to practise on, doesn't it? Tell me, Vanessa, what more do I have to do to inspire your admiration?'

If he thought to make her blush with his silky invitation he had another think coming, although it was a struggle to resist a torrid rush of blood to her head. What *more*? Was he smugly waiting for her to say what a wondrous lover she had found him?

'Clean your own shoes, perhaps?' she ventured with poisonous sweetness.

He pulled a sour face. 'Actually I had something a bit more challenging in mind. I'm sure there are far more stimulating things you can find for me to do with my hands,' he replied with a diabolical innocence, this time succeeding in making her pinken. He leaned back in his seat like a sleekly satisfied cat. 'You see, Richard, Vanessa and I actually have a symbiotic relationship which works extremely well for both of us, so if you were hoping to gain a butler for yourself by stirring up discontent you're out of luck.'

Richard gave Vanessa a fond grin. 'I like to think I already have one, thank you.'

Vanessa sensed the body next to her tighten, but there was no hint of anything but lazy humour in the voice that drawled blandly, 'Purely at my pleasure, I feel constrained to point out. I'm the one with first call on her loyal and devoted services and I can truthfully state that she is the most obliging creature I've ever had under me. In fact her eagerness to please gives new meaning to the phrase "the butler did it"....'

His sheer audacity took Vanessa's already ragged breath away. She could see that he was working himself into a dangerous mood, Richard's complacent ignorance acting as a goad rather than the soothing tranquilliser she might have expected it to be.

It seemed to make no difference to him that she had obviously not told a soul about what had happened. *She* knew, and that was enough. Richard was good-natured almost to a fault but he wasn't stupid and even he was going to realise that there was more than light-hearted banter going on here if Benedict continued in the same provocative vein. The trouble was, taken at face value, there was nothing in his comments she could object to without bringing the whole embarrassing business out in the open, she thought wretchedly.

'Her insistence on making beds, for one,' Benedict continued relentlessly. 'I thought that sort of thing was against the butlers' unwritten code of rights but Vanessa seems to invent her own rules as she goes along.'

Richard laughed. 'I believe it's called job flexibility these days. So you approve of her game of musical beds? When she first told me I thought she was mad, but when you think about it it does make a nutty kind of sense.'

Benedict's sharply indrawn breath was audible and there was a distinctly grim edge in his voice as he enquired gently, 'In what way, would you say?'

'Well, for myself, I wouldn't like to swap beds every night, but, as Van pointed out, she's always lived in other people's houses so she's never developed any possessive hang-ups about where she sleeps. And in time-and-motion terms I suppose you can't get more efficient than airing a bedroom in your sleep. I've got a reasonably large place myself and my mother is constantly complaining about the amount of effort it takes to keep the spare rooms from going musty with disuse. I tell her she should take a leaf out of Van's book, but she says that it would be too much like living in a hotel. Of course, Van says that's exactly what she's doing—except she doesn't have to worry about paying the bill!'

Richard laughed again and Vanessa smiled weakly as the laser-like blue gaze, intensified by the glass lenses, swung back in her direction. So now he had his explanation. And without her having to say a word.

'Vanessa can be very witty, although her sense of humour sometimes leaves a bloody lot to be desired,' came the biting reply after a moment's screaming pause, but Richard's attention had already been distracted.

'Oh, Van, I see Nigel Franklin leaving over there— remember I said I wanted a quick word with him about a mare he's sending over tomorrow? Would you mind? I won't be a moment...'

Vanessa was aghast at the prospect of his desertion at such a critical moment. 'Oh, but——'

'Of course we don't mind.' Benedict cut across her stammer. 'Don't worry, Richard, I know how to keep Vanessa well-entertained.'

Vanessa glumly watched him go.

'Perhaps you're not so as well-matched as I thought, after all. Rather thick, isn't he?'

Her dark eyes flared defensively. 'No, just uncomplicated.'

The dark head nodded. 'I see ... you mean boring.'

'He is not boring!'

'Maybe not below table-level, but then, who am I to judge?'

She bridled with fury. 'I was picking up my fork!' she spluttered.

He sipped his whisky, flaunting his scepticism. 'You were hiding from me.'

'Do you blame me?' She made no further attempt to deny it. 'I knew you wouldn't be able to resist...resist...' Her angry words tapered off as his brows arched.

'Expecting you to admit the truth?'

His smug coolness was infuriating. 'Gloating! Ruining my evening with Richard!'

'Is that what I'm doing?'

'Yes!'

She might have known that would please him. His amusement was tinged with malice. 'Don't you think you deserved a salutary lesson in the dangers of lying?'

'I didn't lie...exactly,' she faltered.

'We both know what a specious defence that is,' he dismissed contemptuously. 'You had every opportunity to correct my mistaken impressions and you didn't. Instead you trotted out that ridiculous ghost story to obscure the issue—tried to make me feel so much like a fool that I doubted my own perceptions. Well, now is the time to make good your numerous sly omissions. And let me warn you—you'd better make it very good!'

'Here?' She looked nervously around. The tables weren't very widely spaced and there were quite a few people here whom she knew. Their conversation had already attracted some curious glances and she hated the idea of generating food for local gossip.

'You had your chance in private and you fudged it,' he said unsympathetically. 'How often can I expect to find you in my bed?'

'For heaven's sake, keep your voice down!' agonised Vanessa.

To her chagrin he immediately lowered his voice to a thready whisper, leaning intimately close so that she could hear. 'Why in the hell didn't you just simply explain your nightly gypsy routine to me? You had no qualms about everyone else knowing. Did you think I'd take exception to an unconventional solution to an understandable problem? For God's sake—I'd have been more inclined to congratulate you for taking such good care of my property!'

'It wasn't that simple——' Vanessa hissed back.

'Why? Because I thought you were an expensive call-girl? You should have been flattered, Flynn.'

She recoiled. 'That's such a typically male thing to say!' she said furiously. 'You think a woman who sells the use of her body to strangers is someone I should *envy*? You think prostitutes do what they do for *pleasure*?' Her voice was choked with revulsion. She had been tainted with that acid brush of contempt once before and the mere memory of it was enough to eat into the scars covering the old wounds.

He looked deeply into her smouldering gaze, his fury stilling at what he saw in the uncertain black depths. 'I'm sorry,' he admitted gently. 'That was a stupid thing for me to say. But I wasn't making a serious social comment, I was just trying to get a rise out of you by being flippant.'

The admission didn't calm her. In her mind she was still fighting that helpless sense of oppression. 'I would never prostitute myself,' she denied fiercely. 'Not for anything or anyone...not for any amount!'

'I know.'

He was no longer angry, she realised with a sting of shock, at least not in the way he had been a few minutes ago. Instead there was a steely determination in his steady gaze that made her swallow hard, suddenly wondering how much her knee-jerk reaction had revealed to him.

He went on, adding to her shock by admitting frankly, 'But I can't deny that it's a common male fantasy—to be seduced by a beautiful stranger who conveniently vanishes afterwards—all pleasure and no responsibility. In real life we all know it doesn't happen that way but we don't have to worry about that when we weave our fantasies. After all, sexual fantasy is the safest sex there is. I'm sure that many women enjoy the reverse of that particular male fantasy in the privacy of their own minds——'

'I don't,' Vanessa interrupted stoutly, trying to stop him before the conversation got totally out of hand.

'Oh? Then what's your favourite sexual fantasy, Vanessa?' He leaned his chin on his hand, that steely glint belying his coaxing expression.

'None of your business,' she said stiffly, bewildered by his swift change of tactics. If he was intent on keeping her off-balance he was doing a damned good job.

'It is if I figure in it,' he mocked her.

'Never in a million years!' Vanessa spat out and he laughed softly.

'You must have been disappointed, then, when you woke up so unexpectedly in my arms?'

She had a fleeting flashback to lean, muscled limbs and rampant masculinity. 'But I didn't wake up, did I?'

she said bitterly. 'If I had a fantasy, it certainly wasn't to be preyed upon by some...some unscrupulous *incubus*...'

'Given the state I was in I doubt whether I fitted the profile of a demon lover, either literally or figuratively,' he murmured.

Did he mean that he'd been so carried away with lust, it had all been over in a trice? Strangely, that thought was even more mortifying. Vanessa had punished herself over and over with speculation that he had enjoyed her helpless body at length and at leisure. She had tossed and turned every night, haunted by the wicked images. Oh, God, if you looked at it like that she *was* having sexual fantasies about him!

'That's a rather odd word to use, though—incubus,' he mused thoughtfully. 'Are you sure you're not getting mixed up with something else?'

'I know what an incubus is,' Vanessa snapped. Now he was calling her ignorant on top of everything else!

'So do I. A demon who makes love to sleeping women. Is that what you're accusing me of—taking advantage of you while you slept?'

'I'd been drinking—you must have realised that; if I'd been in my right mind I would never have acted that way——' Out of the corner of her eye she saw Richard turning away from the tubby figure of Nigel Franklin and his two Asian guests.

'Acted what way?' Benedict persisted.

She glared at him, conscious of Richard's approach. 'If I knew that I wouldn't be worrying about it, would I?'

'Worrying about what?' He continued to be deliberately obtuse as he followed her gaze, watching Richard dip and curve between the tables, pausing to murmur a friendly greeting here and there.

'For goodness sake, what do you care?' she said, smiling brilliantly in relief as Richard neared the table.

'You'd be surprised,' Benedict murmured, turning his back on the other man and rising to his feet to block his view of Vanessa's face. 'But you're right, this isn't the time or place. We're too exposed here.' He let her savour her brief taste of freedom before adding succinctly, 'What we need is a bit of natural cover.' He raised his voice and extended his hand. 'Dance?'

Before she could refuse he had reached down and pulled her out from the banquette, whisking her past the surprised Richard and through the archway into the adjoining room. Applying a delicate pressure to her captured elbow, he spun her deftly against his body and began to move to the throbbing music that poured out of discreetly placed speakers. Several young couples were rocking freely to the beat but Benedict ignored them as he wove a more conservative pattern across the floor, one hand cupping her shoulder-blade, the other firmly pressing hers against his chest.

'But I don't want to dance!' she objected, unobtrusively trying to wrest herself out of his grasp, pushing against his shoulder with her free hand.

'Would you rather I invited Richard to join our fascinating reminiscences about our activities in bed?'

Vanessa slumped in his arms, her physical submission contradicting her defiant words. 'You wouldn't!'

His feet slowed. 'Is that a challenge?'

She turned her head and looked grimly past his right ear, searching for retaliation. 'Don't you feel silly, dancing with a woman who's taller than you?' she said sullenly.

'No. It just means I have a better view of your breasts.'

Her head furiously jerked back and she flushed. He wasn't even looking down into her open cleavage; he was mockingly enjoying the bristling outrage on her face.

'Stop trying to make me feel small. Or rather—smaller than I already am,' he added with rather enchanting diffidence. 'I'm not going to let you dominate me mentally as well as physically. We move well together, don't you think?'

Vanessa's wide mouth thinned stubbornly. 'No.'

His thigh slid between hers as he whirled her around. 'Doesn't this bring back delicious memories?'

'Memories?' she echoed hollowly.

'Of the way we moved together in bed.' The arm across her back tensed, drawing her torso closer so that the tips of her breasts brushed his snowy white chest with every step.

'Stop it!' She arched away and only succeeded in thrusting her hips against his in an even more evocative movement.

'You don't remember, do you?' he taunted huskily, his words blending with the low, sexy throb of the music. He laughed, infuriating her with his perception. 'That's why you were so loath to confess...you didn't know what you'd be confessing to. You don't know what you did during your alcoholic blackout, do you, Vanessa?'

'It wasn't a blackout. I don't know what you're talking about——' she ventured wildly.

'I'm talking about your waking up and finding me naked on top of you...'

Her fingernails dug involuntarily into his jacket. 'You weren't on top of me!'

To her horror he grinned wickedly. 'No, that's right— *you* were on top most of the time, weren't you? Hmm, so you *do* remember something?'

He was enjoying himself hugely at her expense, extracting what, if Vanessa had been in a reasonable frame of mind, she might have acknowledged was a truly fitting revenge. But her frame of mind was anything but reasonable.

'I don't remember *anything*, damn you!' She was driven to admit what he wanted to hear through clenched teeth. 'Nor do I wish to!'

'Liar.' His voice was silky with laughter. 'Don't you want to know exactly how much you have to be embarrassed about? How wild and uninhibited you were in the seamless dark...?'

'No,' she lied fiercely. 'As far as I'm concerned the whole thing was a ghastly mistake. OK, so it was me. I was there, I did whatever you say I did. Now you've got your damned confession we can consider it over and done with,' she gritted.

'Unless you're pregnant.'

'What?' she screeched, stopping dead still in the middle of the dance-floor as if she had been pole-axed. She stared at him in disbelief.

'You mean we didn't——? You didn't even——?' Her mouth quivered with horror as she breathed, 'Oh, God, I don't believe this!' It had never occurred to her that a cautious man like Benedict Savage would not have taken every precaution... and then some!

'I take it this means you're not on the Pill,' he murmured gravely, nudging her back into motion.

'Of course I'm not!' She moaned softly, her body weakly moulding to his as she grappled with this utterly appalling new relevation.

'No, "of course" about it. A lot of women prefer to take responsibility themselves——'

'But I wasn't responsible that night, was I?' she said frantically. 'You must have known I wasn't!'

'How? It was pitch-dark and what you whispered in my ear wasn't exactly calculated to inspire reasoned conversation——'

'Couldn't you smell the wine on my breath?' said Vanessa hurriedly, eager not to hear what she had said.

'Smell, no—taste, yes. But then, you tasted equally intoxicating all over—by the time I got to linger in your mouth I was raging drunk myself...'

Vanessa felt a blush sweep over her from head to toe and quickly got back to the main point. 'How could you

take such a risk, with someone you didn't even
know——?'

'Oh, Dane assured me you had a certificate of health.'

'He *what*?' She trod on his toe and he winced.

'It turned out he meant the car, remember? Only at
the time I thought he was talking about you, you see,
so...'

'So you didn't use anything! How *could* you? Didn't
you *care* that I might—might——?'

'Have my baby? I'm afraid I was so stunned when I
got into bed and found a warm, willing body waiting
for me that I completely lost my head. And you certainly didn't give me any opportunity to politely excuse
myself...'

'Oh—my—God!' Her head bowed, sinking on to his
shoulder. He tightened his grip still further, supporting
her trembling body. Her only consolation was that it
was unlikely that she would have fallen pregnant at what
had been a low point in her monthly cycle. Still, she now
faced weeks of horrible uncertainty.

'If you *are* pregnant I suppose Wells will insist on your
having tests——'

'What?' Her head jerked up again.

Benedict smiled into her pale, frowning face. 'To see
whether the baby is his or mine. After all, I don't suppose
either of us would want to claim the other's child. Shall
we ask him for his opinion when we get back to the
table?'

Her nerveless feet tangled again with his and this time
it was her foot that was momentarily crushed. Benedict
came to a halt.

'Sorry. Have you had enough of dancing? Shall we
go back to Wells?' He began to draw away from her
politely and Vanessa reacted instinctively.

'No!' She practically flung herself against his lean
strength, unconsciously leading as she forced him back
into the safety of motion. She couldn't face Richard yet,

not after the way she had flirted madly with him earlier. The beautiful meal congealed like a block of concrete in her stomach at the very thought of him discovering that she had casually slept with someone else during the time she had been acting like a nervous virgin with Richard. 'No... the music's still playing...'

He meekly followed her agitated footsteps, making no attempt to hide his amusement. 'Poor Vanessa, torn between two lovers...'

'We are *not* lovers!' she denied automatically.

'Then what would you call us?'

'Not *us*!' she blurted confusedly. Unfortunately his intelligence was equal to her confusion. He comprehended instantly what she hadn't meant him to know.

'My God, hasn't the stud performed for you yet?'

'He is *not* a stud!' she bit out.

'Apparently not.' He sounded so smug that Vanessa wanted to hit him. 'Who's been holding back—you or he?'

'Richard and I have had an excellent relationship for two years,' she said sharply. 'Just because it isn't based on sex, it doesn't mean it's not intense——'

'Mmm, it must be intensely unexciting,' he agreed glibly and she struggled not to scream. She tried to ignore the slow slide of the hand between her shoulder-blades down the length of her tingling spine. It wasn't until his hand stopped, his fingers splayed across her lower back, curving against the rise of her buttocks, that she found the breath to reply.

'We're both cautious people,' she said blindly, and promptly threw caution to the winds. 'In fact, we're probably going to get married in the not-too-distant future!'

They moved in silence for a few tense seconds. She could feel his eyes crawling over her averted profile.

'He's asked you to be his wife?'

She bit her lip. 'No, not yet, but——'

'But since you've slept with me you've been feeling so guilty about not sleeping with Richard that you've decided it's time to spice up that "excellent relationship" and see if you're sexually compatible enough to marry him when he does ask,' he guessed with devastating accuracy. 'Is that the reason for the sexy-looking dress you're wearing tonight? A tacit signal that you're on heat at last? And where does that leave me? In the role of a "teaser" I suppose, although I thought they were used to arouse hesitant stallions rather than reluctant mares.'

'How dare you?' she spluttered, hating him for reducing her uncertainties to barnyard analogies.

'Very easily, my dear Flynn,' he drawled. 'Just think of me as saving you a lot of wasted energy. If there's been no sign of spontaneous combustion between Richard and you so far, then no amount of desperate fanning is going to create the missing spark.'

'You're talking about sex, not love——'

'You love him?'

She refused to dignify his impertinent surprise with an answer and stared resolutely away from him.

'Vanessa, look at me.' His hand released hers to take her chin in an unpleasantly firm grasp. He turned her face so that she looked fully into his. 'Do you love him?' he demanded, his expression so intent with serious concern that she was momentarily stunned.

'I—yes.'

She was afraid her hesitation had betrayed her, and to cover it she said aggressively, 'I suppose you're going to say that if I loved him I never would have betrayed him by having sex with you, no matter how drunk I was?'

The soft pad of his thumb stroked the corner of her mouth. 'No, actually I wasn't,' he said gently. 'I don't think I have to tell you anything about your feelings for Wells that you don't already know, deep down inside yourself. It's the strength of your own doubts that's the real betrayal, not anything you might or might not have done with me...'

'Oh, and you think you know me that well, of course,' she said with distinctly shaky sarcasm.

'I know that you need to be loved with a reckless abandon and Wells isn't a man prone to recklessness or, from what I've observed, abandon. He's too tame for you. He'll disappoint you, Vanessa, and not only in bed.'

'Damn you, who in the hell do you think you are? I don't have to take this from you!' whispered Vanessa angrily, dismayed at the ease with which he rifled her private thoughts.

'Thinking of quitting on me, Flynn?' he said as the music died around them. 'I wouldn't advise it.'

She flung back her head defiantly. 'Why not?'

'Because if you do I'll make damned sure that you don't have your tame Richard to run to,' he said with silky menace. 'I think he'll appreciate being made a fool of even less than I did.'

Vanessa paled. 'You mean you'd tell him?'

'Not only him. You know what they say, my dear; a lie has no leg but a scandal has wings. I can just imagine the titillating headlines the tabloids could concoct if they got wind of the true identity of the lascivious ghost of Whitefield Inn. Why, we'd open to roaring trade and you'd be the media's latest darling. Shall we return to your ardent swain? I see him looking rather anxiously this way and I wouldn't like him to get the wrong idea, would you...?'

CHAPTER SEVEN

BARELY fifteen minutes later Vanessa was numbly allowing herself to be put into the passenger seat of Benedict's BMW.

Even while a detached part of her brain despised herself for her meekness she seemed unable to fight the old sense of helplessness that had come flooding back at his final verbal thrust on the dance-floor.

When he had taken her back to the table, propelling her blind progress with an iron hand in the middle of her back, Richard had instantly been concerned.

'Vanessa? What is it? You look as white as a sheet!'

'I feel ill,' Vanessa had replied thickly, her dark eyes unconsciously pleading. 'I want to go home.'

'Of course; let me get the bill——' Richard had risen to his feet, extending an anxious hand only to find her moved firmly beyond his grasp.

'No need to rush, Wells. I'll take her home with me. No sense in your making an unnecessary trip. Say goodnight to Richard, Vanessa.'

Even through the veil of her shock Vanessa had sensed the deep satisfaction in the man beside her as he began to draw her away from the table. He was enjoying thwarting all Richard's expectations of a romantic end to the evening.

'Goodnight, Richard,' she'd repeated mechanically.

A scandal has wings... Vulture's wings. She could feel them beating over her defenceless head.

Only when they'd reached the BMW parked on the gravel by some huge pohutukawa trees did Vanessa summon the presence of mind to protest. 'I had a coat——'

'We'll pick it up some other time. They'll keep it safe. Here, take this if you're cold.' He shouldered out of his white jacket, placing it around her trembling shoulders, enveloping her in his warmth and male scent. He opened the door and tucked her fluid skirt over her thighs when it slipped sideways as she swung her legs inside.

'Are you all right?' he asked as he got in beside her and switched on the headlights.

'Yes,' she clipped, looking through the front windscreen at the way the lights were blurred by the faint mist that was drifting in from the Firth of Thames.

He swore under his breath. 'Damn it, stop looking like that. If he really means that much to you I'll take you back inside!'

The rawness in his tone pierced her numbness.

'Who?' She turned her head. His white shirt shimmered in dimness, the dark tie a slash across his throat; what she could see of his expression was tight and angry.

He gave a coldly exultant laugh at her blank puzzlement. 'No, he doesn't, does he?'

He leaned closer to her, so that she could see the fierce glitter in his eyes. 'What is it you're thinking about, then, Vanessa? Where's all that glorious fight gone? What are you hiding? Or should I say, what is it you're hiding *from*?'

That jolted her. Fight? Dear God, she was just beginning to realise how weaponless she was where he was concerned. 'I don't know what you're——'

'Don't! Don't lie to me!' he cut across her sharply. 'I've had enough of it. You know, I always wondered what it was that made you bury your personality under all those layers of stifling pseudo-obedience..."Yes, sir, no, sir, three bags full, sir." And don't hand me that crap about being content with your job. Maybe you were once, but since the judge died you've enjoyed ruling the roost here by yourself too long and too much to relinquish your independence easily to me or to anyone else. I think you're only just beginning to discover your potential. You want something more out of life, but for some reason you're too afraid to reach out and take it——'

She felt too battered to fend off his quiver of questions; she could only stonewall. 'Not everyone has your single-minded ambition——'

'Had,' he corrected ominously. 'You'll be pleased to note I'm rapidly diversifying my interests. At least I look to the future rather than the past for my solutions. That's why you prefer to steep yourself in history, because it's safe, isn't it, Vanessa? No surprises. History can't hurt you. Only what happens in the present can do that.'

She gave a short, painful laugh. What was in the past could very well hurt you, haunt you; she was living proof of the fact.

Her hand crept to her throat, pressing there to halt the rise of burning bile.

A scandal has wings... How aptly that described the way that lies flew from lip to lip, like the innocent childish whispering game, where the distortion of the original message as it progressed further from the source resulted in great amusement. Except that there had been nothing innocent or amusing in the vicious distortions spread about Vanessa. They had had a very serious intent—to destroy her reputation and undermine her credibility.

Unexpectedly his voice gentled. 'I'm sorry if I frightened you with that stupid threat. You must know that it was only my anger talking. I would never betray you like that. I don't want a scandal any more than you do; I enjoy my privacy too much. You can tell me anything... anything at all. I won't be shocked...'

She almost responded to that soft, enticing invitation, almost weakened, almost trusted him, but then she looked into his eyes, saw the ruthless curiosity there, and instinctively shrank from it. For a moment, in his place, she saw other hungry eyes, avid for her version of 'the truth', promising justice but delivering whatever served them best.

'I won't be shocked'. No, given his worldly sophistication he probably wouldn't be, but the sordid little story still had the power to shock Vanessa, to make her feel again that writhing self-contempt and crippling sense of vulnerability.

'I feel ill,' she said through stiff lips.

'Vanessa——'

'If you don't get me home I'll probably be sick in the car,' she said with bitter relish and he hastily turned the keys in the ignition, expressing his frustration with a loud gunning of the engine as he pulled out into the road.

'Don't think this is the end of it, Flynn,' he brooded as they surged forward into the darkness.

'Make up your mind,' she muttered sullenly.

'What do you mean?'

She risked a glance at his dark profile. His hearing was as acute as his perception. 'You call me Vanessa when you want something and Flynn to threaten me. To put me in my place.'

'I have yet to discover what your place is,' he said cryptically. 'Now, be a good girl and shut up while I concentrate. It's been a bloody long night.'

She remembered then where he had been and felt a small flicker of reviving malice. 'Who beat you for the award?'

A flash of light from an oncoming car revealed a sardonic curl to his lip. 'That pleases you, doesn't it—the thought that I didn't win?'

'Of course not.'

'One day I'm going to teach you to stop telling me lies,' he clipped. 'You like the idea of my pride being trampled in the dust. For your information I didn't nominate myself, Dane did. And I didn't lose.'

'But you said——'

'I didn't say anything; your prancing stud made the assumptions. I told you he was a bit thick.'

'You can't blame him!' She flew to Richard's defence. 'You didn't appear to be in a very celebratory mood.'

'I was until I found my butler hiding under his table,' he said grimly, 'and discovered why.'

Vanessa shivered at the reminder and hugged his jacket more tightly around her. He had a one-track mind. 'If you won, why on earth did you leave early?'

'What should I have done? Stayed to be smothered under the avalanche of sycophantic flattery that goes hand in hand with these things? Is that what you think is important to me? It isn't the first award I've won and it won't be the last. I know exactly how much and how little they really mean.'

Vanessa would have taken issue with that breath-taking piece of arrogance except that she knew that in his case it was justifiable. She had seen a photograph of his array of plaques and awards in one of the *Architectural Digests* and read his offhand comment that winning was 'good for business'.

'But your plans. You were going to stay overnight at the apartment——'

'I changed my mind—I know you think I'm rigid and inflexible but I *am* capable of acting spontaneously on occasion,' he said irritably. 'Maybe I just wanted to celebrate my victory with someone who had no axe to grind, about whose opinion I might actually give a damn!'

There was a fraught silence while Vanessa dared to consider what that meant. He couldn't be talking about *her*? While she sought for a delicate way of finding out he made another impatient sound.

'I might have known you wouldn't be impressed. I suppose you'd prefer to think of me as a valiant loser.

As a disappointed man I'm less of a threat, an object of compassion rather than any positive emotion.'

'Don't be silly——'

'Why not? I've already made a fool of myself over you once.'

'This is ridiculous——'

'I agree, totally absurd.' He stopped the car with a skidding jerk and unclipped his seatbelt to turn towards her.

She stiffened, fighting off a dangerous pleasure, all her senses focused on the man now lifting his arm to rest along the back of her seat. He had come back because of her. Because of some boyish desire to impress her with his cleverness ... Benedict Savage, who took his enormous successes with cynical casualness, had been proudly bearing his honours home on his shield. She moistened her lips and asked nervously, 'Why have we stopped?'

He was silent for a long moment. Then the furious tension that gripped him seemed to relax. 'So that I can seduce you on a dark and lonely street, Vanessa; why else?'

His words sent a wave of heat rolling over her. 'I—— Oh!' She looked out of the window and was mortified to see that they were parked on the gravelled driveway at Whitefield, right before the front door. And she hadn't even noticed! 'Oh.'

'Disappointed?'

She blushed, groping awkwardly for the door-handle and rattling it desperately when she discovered it wouldn't open.

'It's still locked,' Benedict pointed out.

'I realise that,' she said, her damp fingers slipping in panic on the lock as she tried to disengage it.

'Vanessa——'

She heard the rustle of his movement and whirled round in her seat, only to discover that she was still trapped by her seatbelt and that he was leaning across her to deal deftly with the recalcitrant lock.

'What?' To make up for the sharpness of her response she subsided in her seat, reassured by his obvious willingness to let her go.

'Aren't you going to ask me what the award was for?'

'Oh, yes—what was it for?' she asked hurriedly, feeling ashamed of the self-absorption that had led her to misjudge his motives so blatantly badly.

'Are you really interested?'

Typical of the male injured ego—he was going to make her work for his forgiveness. 'Of course.'

'I thought you didn't like my work.'

'Who told you that?'

'Dane. When he was here last year you told him that you thought the Serjeant Building was a boring monolith, exhibiting the kind of concrete-slab mentality that made modern cities universally the same.'

'He just showed me a photo and asked my opinion,' she said weakly, remembering the amusement the other man had displayed when she had unwisely abandoned her customary reserve around her employer's guests and proffered an honest rather than diplomatic response. 'I didn't realise you had designed it.'

Benedict didn't seem in the least offended. 'One of my earliest commissions, when I was still working for my father's firm. He had a stern rule that one supplied clients with what they wanted, not what the architect thought they should want. In that case the client was a hidebound reactionary who thought that Frank Lloyd Wright was a dangerous lunatic. That building fitted him like a second skin.'

'I don't mind some of your later designs,' Vanessa said comfortingly.

'Thank you for that damningly faint praise,' he said wryly. 'I realise commercial architecture is largely a soulless business...precisely because it's such a *big* business, cost-driven to the point that anything new and untried or unusual is usually feared. Plans often have to be approved by a board, and committees are notoriously more conservative and difficult to please than individuals. Only those with real foresight, who want to make a permanent impact on the landscape rather than a smooth turn-around profit on construction, are interested in allowing an architect full artistic freedom. That's why I left my father's firm and branched out with Dane. I wanted to create a separate professional identity for myself...concentrate on smaller commissions calling for greater individualism. I still do the big——' a taunting semi-bow to Vanessa '—"boring" bread-and-butter ones, but these days I supplement the stodge with a good leavening of the off-beat. The award was for a private residence at Piha. Would you like to see it?'

'Go to Piha, you mean?' Vanessa was startled.

His white teeth flashed in the darkness. 'I was talking about something a little more convenient—the plans are up in my studio.'

'Oh. Yes, that would be very interesting,' she murmured, trying and failing to imagine what kind of houses Benedict Savage would design.

Palatial homes for millionaires and pillars of society, no doubt—they were probably the only ones who could afford his magnificent fees. But at least his dangerous mood seemed to have evaporated now that she had given his ego room to flex. 'I'd like to see it, some time when it's convenient . . .'

His eyes glittered as if he sensed he was being 'handled'. 'I'd better put the car in the garage. Would you like to open up the house? And here, you may as well take this.'

He scooped up something from the back seat and thrust a cool, metallic object into her hands. She found herself looking down at a slender, stylised sculpture. 'Oh, is this your award? It's very nice.'

She heard the smile in his voice. 'Yes, very nice. Run on in, there's quite a chill outside. Have you got your key?'

'I'm not a child.' She opened her door to get out and found herself pulled up with a jerk that made her gasp with pain.

'Here, allow me.' Kindly, Benedict freed her from her seatbelt and she scrambled out in a flurry of black crêpe de Chine, still clutching his jacket around her, conscious of his chuckle pursuing her up the steps.

She was acting like a nervous teenager for no reason at all, she simmered as she flicked on the lights in the foyer and stairwell. He must have known that she thought he was going to pounce on her. But then, what was she supposed to think after the things he'd said to her at the restaurant? Beneath the challenging interplay of words there had run a definite current of sexual awareness, heightened by his obviously vivid recollection of their lovemaking.

Unconsciously she placed a hand over her flat stomach. He had actually sounded quite smug when he'd raised the question of pregnancy, as if the idea of her bearing his child wasn't at all dismaying. In little more than a week he had invaded her body and wrapped himself around her consciousness to such an extent that the certainties that had been her strength and her protection over the last few years had begun to crumble. She was losing control and somehow she had to find a way to regain it.

She put the award carefully on the hall table beside the telephone after studying the engraved plague and was still hovering there uncertainly when Benedict slipped through the front door, which she had left ajar. He must have parked the car with remarkable speed, she thought as he closed the door behind him and locked it, then leant back against the stripped-wood panels just looking at her.

She moved restlessly under that steady gaze. 'I was just wondering whether you wanted me to serve you coffee——' She faltered as he pushed away from the door and began to walk slowly towards her. Automatically she backed away, until she reached a wall and could retreat no further.

It took all her will-power not to shrink back as he came to an unsmiling halt in front of her and reached out to unhitch his jacket from her shoulders with a single finger and draw it away. The slippery silk lining slid down over her bare arms like a caress. He tossed the jacket over the elaborately carved newel post at the bottom of the stairs and casually leaned against the wall, his hand planted beside her tense shoulder.

'Now who's trying to put whom in their place?' he mocked softly. 'After tonight you won't ever dare call me sir again. Get used to it, Vanessa.'

'Used to what?' Her eyes were slightly higher than his but she felt small and surrounded.

'The new relationship between us. If you're going to run this inn for me, you're going to have to do it with authority. You have to decide whether you want to be a butler for the rest of your life or whether you're ready to move on and up.'

'Me? Run the inn?' Vanessa said faintly, pressing herself back against the supporting wall to try and escape the heat of his body.

He had loosened the black tie on the way in from the car and unbuttoned the top pearl stud of his shirt. The white pleated shirt was so thin, she could see the shadow of his torso outlined through the silk. His chin was dark with regrowth. He looked tired, disordered, and disturbingly sexy. It was incredible, but this man, with his only mildly good looks and his spectacles and his studied emotional colourlessness, harboured a smouldering sexuality that was as electrifying as it was astonishing. Vanessa was bewildered. Why had she never

seen it before? And why, now that she could see it was
so obvious, wasn't he smothered in women wherever he
went?

His eyebrows rose. 'Isn't that what you had in mind
when you suggested a manager?'

She shook her head. 'No, it never occurred to me!'

'Not even in your secret dreams?'

Her eyes slid away from his. She had no intention of
telling him what her secret dreams involved. 'How could
I?' she asked huskily. 'I don't know anything about
running a hotel——'

'The job you're doing now isn't so far removed from
it,' he pointed out quietly. 'You provide accommodation
services for my guests, manage staff and purchase
supplies. You do accounts and supervise building and
maintenance. I think you'd be surprised how well-
equipped you are for the job. A small hotel like this needs
an intimate, highly individualistic management style,
preferably by someone attuned to its unique atmosphere. Who better than you? You love it here, don't you?
Wouldn't you like to know that you didn't have to leave?
That you could stay on and build it into something that
we can both be proud of? If you feel inadequate in any
way, there are always courses you can take to improve
your management skills...'

It was such a powerfully seductive offer that Vanessa
was afraid to question the motives behind it.

'Why me?'

'Because I'm already used to having you around.'

'Oh.'

She was convenient. That hurt and she lowered her
lashes against him. From the corner of her eye she
watched his free hand move up to finger the velvety loop
on the open edge of the neckline which lay against her
collarbone, his knuckles almost brushing her chin, and
he continued, softly chiding, 'You should be flattered.
I don't let people into my life very easily. My mother

elevated emotional manipulation to an art form, and to this day I still have a natural disinclination to trust my feelings for fear they'll be used against me, particularly where women are concerned. I think we're alike in that respect—slow to trust—which is why I'm willing to forgive you for playing games with my head. I realise you were only trying to protect yourself. But I'm offering you a unique opportunity here and the beauty of it is, you don't even have to leave home to take advantage of it.'

His finger counted down to the next empty loop and the next, not touching anything but the fabric and yet managing to make her feel as if her skin was being brushed by a thin trickle of fire. At her sharply indrawn breath he looked up from his fascinating tracery and murmured persuasively, 'I do trust you, you see. Will you trust me? If not as a man then at least as a businessman. I'll be totally honest with you, Vanessa. I'd very much like to have you back in my bed, but neither offer is contingent upon your accepting the other. Whether we become lovers or not has no bearing on the fact that I think you're the perfect person to run the inn. I won't make it difficult for you if you choose to make profit with me rather than love, and I certainly won't attempt any emotional manipulation. Ask Dane—I might not like losing, but I'm graceful in defeat.'

His finger flicked down the rest of the open loops to wedge into the fabric V where the bodice was fastened between her breasts and he paused before adding slyly, 'Although you may have to bear with me a little; I'm so rarely defeated that I might be a little rusty about my graces...'

Her mouth came open but nothing issued forth from her parted lips. She was very conscious that the boning of her bodice had made wearing a bra unnecessary and wondered if he had guessed. Her breasts rose and fell, the inner slopes caressing his relaxed finger. He watched

the expressions flitting across her face with a faint smile
and delicately curved the other fingers of his hand under
the smooth edge of the bodice, rubbing his thumb lightly
over the top of the fabric. The backs of his fingers moved
delicately against the silky swell of her breast in a secret
caress that they were both intensely aware of. Only mil-
limetres away from his touch, the soft, satiny peak
tightened in an agony of anticipation. Blood rushed to
her head, making her feel dizzy with unimagined
pleasure.

'This is a very elegant, sexy dress. It looks as if it's
melting over you,' he purred, bending a knee so that it
touched hers through the folds of her skirt.

'I made it myself,' she heard herself whisper inanely,
thinking that it was what was under the dress that was
melting.

'Resourceful Vanessa.' His praise curled around her
ears and stroked across her senses. 'Your hands are obviously as quick and clever as your tongue.'

She blushed right down into her cleavage and he
laughed huskily, his whisky-warm breath teasing her
mouth.

'I was complimenting you on your wit, Nessa. What
did you think I meant?'

'Exactly what you wanted me to think,' she said, simultaneously hot with excitement and shivery with fear.

Benedict probably thought she was able to hold her
own with this kind of dangerous sexual banter but
Vanessa knew she was already in over her head. The only
other time she had tried it she had been badly hurt. What
had started out as a seduction in which she had willingly
participated had become little better than rape when
Julian St Clair had become brutally impatient with her
inexperience. Her slowness to respond to his physical
cues had made him lose his temper and abandon any
further attempts to arouse her.

He had taken what he wanted and left her bleeding and in pain, telling her flatly that virgins were more trouble than they were worth. This despite the fact that her innocence was what had attracted him in the first place. He had deliberately set out to make her fall in love with him and then abandoned her as just another of life's challenges that hadn't lived up to his jaded expectations.

'I don't know what happened between us so you shouldn't tease me about it,' she said uneasily. 'It's not fair.'

His fingers stilled their delicate by-play. 'Does that worry you?'

She swallowed, pulling her mind back to the present. Benedict wasn't anything like Julian. For one thing he was older and more discriminating, a man who had achieved brilliant success on his own terms, not a spoiled, idle playboy trading on his family name. And he was as patient as he was tenacious, as demanding on himself as on others. He wouldn't hurt her, not physically, anyway...

'Of course it worries me...'

He sighed, and to her aching disappointment withdrew his hand from her dress. He removed his glasses and hung them carelessly from his hip pocket, then curved his fingers around her throat as he looked deep into her eyes. Once again, she succumbed to the spell of his mesmerising gaze.

'I'm sorry,' he murmured meaninglessly as he applied gentle pressure to the nape of her neck, drawing her down to his mouth.

She couldn't have resisted even if she had wanted to; the mysterious shadows in those deep blue eyes were simply too alluring. They made her want to know who the man really was behind his self-controlled mask, to find out whether the strange, shivery sensations that radiated through her body at his lightest touch were real or merely the illusion of desire. She forgot that he was her employer, that there were very sound and sensible reasons why this should not be allowed to happen. She drifted into his embrace with a thrilling knowledge of her own daring. *He* hadn't been disappointed in her as a lover... She had obviously pleased him and now it was time to discover if he pleased her!

It wasn't the fierce, hungry kiss sizzling with passion that Vanessa had eagerly expected, but a long, slow kiss of silky exploration...so long that she nearly suffocated in sweetness before he released her to breathe, only to draw her in again, to taste her with luscious bites of erotic pleasure, his teeth sinking into her swollen lower lip, his tongue unfurling inside her to stroke and linger. A lovely, sensual lethargy dragged at her lower limbs. Her arms slid around his waist to cling to the only solid support in a world of dissolving bliss. She had never known there were so many ways to kiss.

'Why are you sorry?' she whispered in blurred tones as his mouth shifted to the side of her throat and slid lower to the little hollow where her pulse fluttered madly. Her breasts were hurting against his chest, tight and unbelievably tender. When was he going to touch her there again?

Instead his arm slid around her back and he drew her away from the wall as if they were dancing, his mouth still moving against her long, slender neck as he swayed towards the stairs. 'Come with me...'

'Where?' It was a dreamy request, without force or curiosity. She knew where he was taking her. Up to heaven in his arms.

'You'll see...'

He wafted her slowly up into the darkness of the upper floor, stair by stair, kiss by kiss, as if he was afraid that if he let her go for a moment the sensual spell he was weaving would be broken, but, instead of ending up in his bedroom, when he finally wrenched himself away with a soft groan of regret she found herself blinking owlishly in the harsh fluorescent lighting of his studio.

Dazed and trembling, she reached out, but he was already turning away and unrolling something across the draughting-table and clipping the edges flat. His hands, she was glad to see, were shaking as much as hers.

'What are you doing?'

'I want you to see this. The perspective drawings that won the award. And photos of the finished house.'

She stared at him incredulously. He wanted to talk about his work, *now*? 'Ben...'

'Please.' The look he gave her was both searing and pleading. 'It's important to me.' He held out his hand, steady now, and when she took it he drew her hard against his side, his other hand curving possessively over her hip as he firmly directed her attention to the board.

'You see—it's built on a steep hillside covered with native bush. For a couple and their three children. They're both artists. He works with stained glass—that's why there's so much used in the design; they wanted a sense of the bush behind drawn inside the house rather than pushed away by four solid walls. And they didn't have much money, so I had to incorporate a lot of odds and ends that they'd rescued from demolition sites and make sure that a lot of the building work was do-it-yourself capable. What do you think?'

She could hardly think at all, her whole body attuned to the thumb that was stroking her hipbone through the slippery black fabric, but he seemed anxious, so she struggled for a response that would earn his approval. Then, as her interest was caught, she didn't have to struggle at all.

'Why, it's lovely.' She bent over to study the higgledy-piggledy juxtaposition of shapes, the way the house seem to mimic the uneven growth patterns of the surrounding bush, taking on odd tilts and angles obviously to avoid the necessity for cutting down the mature trees scattered over the site. 'It's *fantastic*!' She turned dark, astonished eyes to his. 'You did *this*?'

'I should be insulted by that disbelieving look,' he drawled unsteadily, his expression strangely grave. 'But yes, I did that, although you'll notice it's not signed Savage. I use another professional name for this kind of work, what I call the fun stuff. It's a way for me to let off steam, to indulge myself and yet not compromise Dane Benedict's reputation with our conservative corporate clients... although my identity's no secret in the trade.'

'What are these here?' Vanessa was fascinated by the loving intricacy of his detail. Compared to the slick, water-colour washed sketches of his award-winning commercial work that she had seen these were like illustrations rather than designs, maps of the imagination. 'They look like ladders up the walls. Where do they go? Are these lofts——?'

'Play-lofts and tunnels between the children's rooms.' He gave them a quick, uninterested glance and then deliberately put his hand down over the section she was trying to interpret. 'Vanessa, I didn't bring you here to play twenty questions. I just wanted you to see it, that's all. So that you'd realise that I am capable of being... whimsical and sensitive to interpreting other people's needs, even if they're not completely sure about them themselves. I mean, I may come across as a heartless bastard sometimes but——'

'I never thought you were that——' Vanessa was driven to protest, the lovely warmth of passion beginning to drain away. Was he trying to let her down lightly? To explain that he had responded to her only because he thought that she had needed the flattery of his desire?

'Until now.'

'What's that supposed to mean?' she asked hollowly, not wanting to know the answer.

He turned her, holding her at arm's length by her shoulders, his face grim. 'Just this: unless you lied about sleeping with Wells or have some other secret lover hidden away, there's no way you can be pregnant.'

For a moment she was puzzled and then she realised what he was admitting and why he looked so tense, almost anguished.

'Oh, Benedict, I'm so sorry...' Had he thought that she would think him less of a man because of it? She stroked his taut mouth with tender compassion and he recoiled as if her finger were tipped in poison.

'*You're* sorry?'

'Are you quite certain?' she asked, seeing that she had jolted him with her swift understanding. 'There's a lot that doctors can do about sterility these days——'

He dropped his hands from her shoulders, his eyes blazing with cobalt fire. 'What in the hell are you talking about? I'm not sterile!'

He sounded so furiously certain that Vanessa's heart squeezed in her chest. 'You have children?' She faltered. It had never even occurred to her. Oh, she was so *naïve*!

'No, I *don't* have children!' he shouted at her, so furiously offended that she took a step back.

'Then—then how do you know you're not sterile?' she stammered with what she felt was impeccable logic.

'Because——' He stopped and uttered a word that made her pinch her mouth primly. 'I don't *know*—all right? But I have no reason to *not* believe I'm not——' He ran a hand through his hair in an uncharacteristic gesture of helplessness. 'Oh, hell, will you stop confusing the damned issue while I'm trying to make a confession?'

'*I'm* confusing it?' Vanessa couldn't help an involuntary smile, which seemed to infuriate him beyond bearing. She had never seen him so close to losing control. It was quite fascinating.

As she watched, round-eyed, he took a deep, controlling breath and said very, very carefully, 'What I'm *trying* to tell you, Vanessa, is that there is not the ghost of a chance that I got you pregnant that night——' It was a measure of his mood that there wasn't even the glimmer of amused recognition of his inadvertant pun.

'Oh?' Her limited sexual experience sent her imagination haywire. 'You mean you—er—withdrew ... before you ... ?'

'No, I didn't *withdraw*,' he snarled. 'There was nothing for me to have to withdraw *from*.'

Vanessa looked at him, appalled. Her colour rose, along with her vivid curiosity. 'You mean we just ... did it without actually——?'

'We didn't *do* anything in bed that night!' he exploded. 'Correction, we did do *something*,' he amended grimly. 'We slept.'

'Slept?'

He shrugged, easing the motion down through the rest of his body as if loosening it up for combat.

'*Slept*?' She repeated sharply. It was finally beginning to sink in.

'Yes, you know, that state of unconsciousness wherein one is completely relax——'

'We *slept*!'

He bowed his head, awaiting the storm. It wasn't long in breaking.

'Why, you——' Vanessa rounded on him like a furious tornado. 'Are you telling me that I didn't——?'

'Ravish me? I'm afraid not,' he said meekly.

'That you didn't——?'

'Ravish *you*—no.'

'That we just spent the whole time *sleeping*! And you expect me to believe that? What do you think I am, an *idiot*?' she screeched.

'No, an innocent.' He was unwise enough to expand on that. 'If I'd made love to you that night, Vanessa, believe me you would have been in no doubt of it the next morning. You would have been aching and tender in places I'm too polite to mention——'

'You—*polite*?' she spat. 'Was it polite to let me think——? You . . . you *bastard*!' She went bright red at what she had thought. How he must have been laughing at her!

'Tit for tat, Vanessa,' he pointed out, but Vanessa was in no mood to be fair. Her temper had reached flashpoint and her hand had streaked out and cracked across his face before she even realised her intention.

'That's one,' he said so coolly that she lashed out again, across the other cheek. His head snapped to the side with the force of the fresh blow. Slowly he looked back at her.

'That's two.'

She wasn't foolish enough to make it three but she had a desperate need to goad him out of that infuriating calmness.

'What are you trying to do, frighten me?' she sneered, circling him in a swirling of skirts like a black thunderstorm building up static electricity.

He, perversely, seemed to think he had already weathered the worst. He folded his arms across his chest, slowly rotating to follow her prowling progress. 'I don't have to. You're doing a very good job of frightening yourself. I always wondered what you'd look like in a passion. Now I know. You should lose your temper more often.'

She knew he was trying to distract her. 'And you should be ashamed of yourself!' she spat, clenching her hands in the soft folds of her skirt. All the thwarted passion of a few minutes ago was now channelled into the relief valve of rage.

'I think I should be complimented for my honesty,' he protested. 'I'll even admit that I looked and I lusted but the flesh was sadly unwilling.'

Was he trying to tell her that no man would want her, even served up on a platter? She flinched, then rallied furiously. She wasn't going to let him get away with sexually humiliating her. She had promised herself that no man would ever do that again. 'It damned well wasn't unwilling when *I* woke up,' she flung at him. 'You were certainly plenty aroused *then*.'

He had the gall to flaunt a grin. 'I'm usually at my best in the mornings,' he said modestly. 'And I was probably dreaming about what was to come...so to speak. I had every intention of making love to my luscious satin-wrapped present when I'd slept off my jet-lag. I was very disappointed to find her a figment of my lustful imagination.'

'You're disgusting!' choked Vanessa, coping with a rush of conflicting feelings—relief, embarrassment, forbidden delight...

'I'm a man.'

'You're a pervert!'

'The perversion would have been if I'd brought you up here and made love to you without telling you that it was our first time together. It wouldn't have done for us both to discover you were still a virgin——'

'I've made love before!' she flared defiantly.

'Good. Then I won't have to worry about hurting you——'

She shuddered at the painful memory that that evoked, wrapping her arms around her waist and hugging herself in a revealing gesture that made his eyes narrow and his mouth thin.

'Surely you don't have the gall to think that I'd let you—— ' She choked to a halt as he moved closer, his voice gentling.

'Not *let*, Vanessa. Fully participate as a mature adult. Nothing's changed. You wanted me enough to come this far——'

'No, I didn't, I was just curious.'

His mouth thinned still further. 'Was, and still are. Would you like me to prove it to you, Vanessa? At least I've been honest with you. More so than you've been with me...'

'What do you mean?'

'All this outrage about what I did or didn't do to you. Isn't it really a mask for your own guilty feelings? Didn't it secretly excite you to think about how liberated our lovemaking must have been ... neither of us in any state to worry about restraint or inhibition? Weren't you even a little aroused when you woke up to find me beside you?'

She hugged herself tighter. 'I was shocked——'

'Of course you were shocked. But there you were, semi-nude, cuddled up with a naked, aroused man who was completely vulnerable to whatever you chose to do to him. You were curious about me then, too, weren't you, Vanessa? It never occurred to you that it might have been rape, because subconsciously even then you trusted me. So you didn't scream. You looked at me instead. You looked at my body. Did you touch me? Did you *want* to touch me? I would have liked it if you had. I would have liked to have been woken that way, liked it more than anything...'

She couldn't look at him, turning her back and trying to retrieve her badly fragmented composure. 'I——'

'Because I touched you, Vanessa,' he told her with devastating candour as he moved up behind her.

'When I got into bed with you I fondled you a little before I drifted off to sleep—your long, gorgeous back and especially that beautiful, rounded bottom.' His arms came around her body to wrap themselves over hers and gently tug them down to her sides, pressing them there as his voice nuzzled in her hair. 'It was so irresistible...all bare and warm under that flimsy satin slip, like a delicious, downy peach I wanted to bite into... You were lying on your front so I couldn't stroke your breasts, but I knew they must be ripe and full because your slip was loose and I could see the luscious swell at the side where your breast was compressed against the bed. I went to sleep thinking about turning you over and cupping them in my hands, finding out how your nipples would taste, whether they were big or small, cherry-pink or——'

'Stop it!' she cried faintly, far too late for the protest to be effective.

'Why, am I turning you on, Vanessa?' He ran his hands lightly up and down her arms and then, taking her by surprise, spun her around, looking deeply satisfied when he saw her flushed face and cornered eyes, the full lower lip that he had bitten so voluptuously earlier now captured by her own nervous teeth.

He touched her hair with a tenderness that made her eyes sting. 'Don't worry. I'm not going to force you to do anything that you don't want to. Not tonight, anyway. I won't rush you but I'm not going to let you deny your feelings, either, or mine. I give you fair warning that I have every intention of fulfilling my fantasies where you're concerned!'

CHAPTER EIGHT

VANESSA lifted her head and let the stiff breeze float her loosely bound hair off her shoulders. She dug her cold hands deeper into the pockets of her down jacket as she walked along the beach, stepping carefully in her thick-soled trainers to avoid slipping on the piles of loose rocks.

Unlike the silky white-sand beaches of the east coast of the Coromandel, most of the west-coast bays were small, rock-strewn stretches of brown sand scalloped from point to rocky point, the mussel- and oyster-encrusted rocks at the waterline giving way to small boulders than could be overturned to reveal scuttling colonies of crabs and, up past the high-tide line, bleached driftwood and stiffened brown seaweed lay among thick drifts of smoothly weathered stones and pebbles ranging through the spectrum of earth colours.

Vanessa looked up at a sharp cry, but it was only a seagull wheeling above the shallow inshore waters, brown with stirred-up sand. She watched its soaring, wind-tossed flight across the pale grey sky, envying its freedom. There were times she would like to fly free, away from all her problems. But instead she could only drive and walk and even then she wasn't escaping them, because her biggest problem was herself.

She turned to retrace her steps and froze, her heart shuddering in her breast.

Correction, her biggest problem was in front of her, calmly strolling between the rocks as if he had as much right to be there as she did.

She waited until he got into earshot before she asked tightly, 'What are you doing here?'

Benedict shrugged, his black leather jacket sliding open over his cream sweater with the careless movement as he halted on the other side of a shallow rock-pool. 'Walking.'

She snorted. 'You never walk.'

'Only because I don't usually stay here long enough to miss my daily swims. I've decided I'd better get out and about a bit if I don't want to run to fat.'

She gave his lean length a contemptuous look. 'I don't think you have to worry about that.'

'Thank you.'

'It wasn't a compliment, it was a statement of fact,' she said irritably.

'Thank you anyway. You're looking very trim yourself.'

He was looking at her long legs, clad in the jeans that she kept in the boot of the estate car along with her spare down parka and a pair of old sports shoes. When she had left the house earlier she hadn't even bothered to change, just grabbed a cardigan and fled, and now, with her prim navy 'uniform' lying on the back seat of the car, she felt wretchedly defenceless.

She brushed the wind-blown hair out of her eyes, trying to tuck the strands back into the scarf she had used to tie it back.

'Did you follow me here?' she asked bluntly.

'What makes you think that?'

She refused to retreat in the face of his daunting amusement. 'It seems a very strange coincidence, that's all.'

'Since there's only one main road around here, it's not *that* much of a coincidence. I saw the car parked on the verge so I stopped.'

He made it sound like an idle impulse but what reason would he have for driving north from Whitefield? He didn't strike her as a man with sightseeing on his mind. That only left one alternative.

'You said I could have the afternoon off,' she challenged.

'I suggested *we* take the afternoon off,' he corrected gently. 'And you snuck away to hide as soon as my back was turned.'

'I'm not hiding. I just wanted to—to get some fresh air and stretch my legs,' she invented wildly.

Ever since that electric encounter two weeks ago she had been attempting to put a physical distance between them that he had been equally determined to thwart. One night, to her fury, he had invited Richard and his mother to dinner and commanded Vanessa to act as his hostess. She had been forced to smile and act cool and unruffled by his teasing casualness while underneath she had simmered with a temper that had given an unaccustomed sparkle to her looks and prompted some searching glances from Mrs Wells. She couldn't help but be aware, seeing Richard and Benedict together, how dramatically different they were, like light and shadow, day and night, and unfortunately a primitive part of her was far more fascinated by the powerful lure of the hidden and forbidden than the mellow sunshine.

To her further dismay, during dinner Richard had let the cat out of the bag about the work she was doing for Judge Seaton's publisher, completing the book about the colourful history of Thames that he had been working on at the time of his death. Richard had cheerfully recounted the difficulties she had had trying to collate and compress boxes of copious notes and sort through half-scribbled ideas in her spare time and somehow by the end of the meal Vanessa had found that she had been neatly manoeuvred into accepting Benedict's help.

Since then much of her spare time had been spent cheek by jowl with Benedict at the library desk, resolutely trying to treat him like a block of wood while deeply chagrined to realise that his unwelcome expertise was indeed making the book progress much faster.

'Precisely my plan,' he said smugly now. 'We can stretch our legs together. Exercise is boring without company, don't you think?'

'No.'

He regarded her truculent glare with amusement. 'Well, in that case you just carry on by yourself and I'll keep a discreet distance behind.'

'Oh, don't be ridiculous——!'

'It's not me who's being ridiculous, Vanessa,' he said gently. 'What did you think I intended when I suggested you and I play hooky today?'

Vanessa turned away but he had already seen her blush. 'Do I have to tell you my thoughts now? Aren't I entitled to *any* privacy at all?' she demanded fiercely.

'You can have all you want. I haven't brought my thumbscrews with me. In fact, have I *ever* forced a confidence out of you, Vanessa?'

'You're always doing it!' she countered explosively.

'Ah, but by stealth, never by force.'

She gave him a look of immense frustration, aware that he was right. While they had been closeted together over the judge's disordered manuscript she had revealed far more about herself than she had intended, since talking about herself was the only proven way of stemming his tide of threatening confidences about himself.

She didn't want to be lured into curiosity about the velvety-dark contradictions of his character. She certainly didn't want to know that he had worn glasses since he was twelve years old, and that they had fogged up when he had received his first French kiss from a girl when he was fifteen... although she had found herself thinking that perhaps that explained why he had taken them off when he had kissed her!

She didn't *want* to know those other things about him that touched her heart: that his childhood had been restricted by parental expectations to the point of oppression—an imperious father whose rigid, exacting standards of excellence had raised his son to expect nothing less of himself than perfection and a mother whose social expectations of him had been every bit as stringent and repressive. One didn't express emotions openly in the Savage family circle, one acted with dignity at all times. One doled out affection when it was earned by correct behaviour or academic excellence.

Benedict had learned the lessons of his early childhood well. On the surface he had been the perfect son. He had never rebelled as a teenager, he had performed to expectation at school and at home. He had dutifully joined his father's architectural firm when he had graduated from university and carried on the conservative family tradition, regarding homes and possessions and even people as profitable investments rather than emotional attachments.

Underneath, though, other forces had been at work, the intellectual curiosity and ruthlessly competitive ambition that his father had relentlessly encouraged constantly thwarted by the restrictions imposed by his status within the firm. As the years had passed he'd come to realise that his father's expectations for him, far from being infinite, were quite claustrophobically finite—the pinnacle of Benedict's professional success was to be the inheritance of the company when his father retired and his duty then would be the continuation of the Savage dynasty.

By the age of twenty-eight, Benedict had come to a full recognition that he was not the man his father wanted him to be, and never would be. He wanted more and he wanted it on his own terms.

The split had been achieved with customary Savage dignity, a frigid debate in which both men had obdurately refused to compromise. No emotional outbursts, no public washing of dirty linen, merely a cleverly managed PR announcement that had poured cold water on the choice rumours of a family rift. Benedict had continued to see his parents occasionally on a social basis, although he was left in no doubt from his mother that she was deeply disappointed in him and would deny him the warmth of her approval until he had got over his childish fit of rebellion against his father and returned to the family fold.

Benedict had commented wryly that since his mother's approval was never very warm anyway he could live comfortably without it.

However, understanding him more didn't make him any easier for Vanessa to deal with.

'I think I've had enough fresh air now,' she said desperately, and began to march back down the way she'd come.

Predictably, Benedict matched her stride for stride but he was watching her instead of his footing and a rock shifted beneath his leather shoe, causing him to skid off into a small hollow of sea-water, soaking the cuff of his black trousers.

Vanessa, whose hand had darted out instinctively when he stumbled, snatched it away hastily as he smiled warmly at her in gratitude.

'Thank you, Nessa.'

'Walking over rocks in shoes like that is asking for trouble,' she said, quickening her gait to escape the potency of that stunning smile. 'And now I'll have to send those trousers to be dry-cleaned. Why didn't you wear something practical, like jeans?'

'I didn't know what we were going to be doing,' he said equably. 'And I don't own any jeans.'

That seemed so inconceivable to one of her generation that she stared at him in wonder. 'What do you relax in?' Then she remembered who it was she was talking to. 'Oh, yes, that's right; you don't have time to relax.'

'Until now there was no need,' he commented. 'Perhaps you can teach me to relax, Vanessa.'

She ignored him, remaining stubbornly silent until she reached the car. There she halted, frowning as she saw a vaguely familiar wicker hamper sitting by the front wheel.

'Where did that come from?'

'Kate. It's a picnic.'

'Picnic?'

'Kate said you told her you were going to the beach and then took off before she could pack you some lunch. She said you often had sandwiches on the beach when the weather was fine. She thought you might have had things on your mind and just forgot to ask.'

Vanessa cursed the over-developed sense of responsibility that had made it impossible for her to take off without letting someone know where she could be found. However, she welcomed the realisation that the hollowness in the region of her stomach might not be entirely due to Benedict's unsettling effect on her nervous system.

'I'm not hungry.'

His look was one of amused scepticism. 'Well, I am, so you can just sit and watch me eat before we go.'

'We?' She suddenly noticed that hers was the only car parked along the whole foreshore. 'Where's your car?'

'One of the plasterers dropped me off. He lives at Tapu and was going home for lunch.'

'You took a lot for granted, didn't you?'

'I didn't think you'd be callous enough to drive off and leave your employer stranded.'

Her eyes narrowed. 'Is that a threat?'

'Your paranoia is showing. For goodness' sake, Vanessa, what do you think I can do to you on a public beach?'

He picked up the hamper and began walking towards a huge, twisted pohutukawa tree whose gnarled branches overhung a steep grassy bank below the curve of the road. After a moment she reluctantly followed.

By the time she reached him, deliberately dawdling, Benedict had shaken out a blanket over the long, springy grass.

'I hope you're not going to loom over me the whole time I eat. Sit down. Learn to relax, Vanessa,' he mocked as he sat down on the blanket and shrugged out of his jacket before beginning to rustle about in the hamper.

She sat, and was instantly aware of a strange sense of isolation. With their combined weight the blanket was compressed startlingly deep into the surrounding grasses so that only the sea down the slope directly in front of them remained open to their view. They were totally private from the rest of the beach and the road above. It was also surprisingly warm out of the direct bite of the wind, so warm that Vanessa unzipped her parka and peeled it off, straightening her fleecy grey angora cardigan as she did so.

'Just like a cosy little nest in here, isn't it?' Benedict murmured, echoing her thoughts with unnerving accuracy. 'And look at you. Downy as a young chick. Would you like coffee or champagne?'

She looked at the cut-crystal glass and Royal Doulton cup he was offering, and then at the silver cutlery and starched white linen napkins he had laid on the undulating surface of the blanket. Nothing but the best for Benedict Savage. Always.

'Coffee, please,' she said primly.

'That's right, must keep a clear head,' he said blandly, producing a stainless-steel Thermos flask and pouring a steaming stream of coffee into the cup. 'Milk and sugar, m'lady?'

'No, thank you.'

He handed her a cup and poured one for himself before unwrapping some of the food, which was far more practical than the luxury accoutrements, thought Vanessa in amusement. Kate knew what made a good picnic, no matter how wealthy you were: bacon-and-egg pie; marinated cold chicken; creamy, golden New Zealand cheddar; thick, crusty home-made bread and pickles that Vanessa remembered helping to bottle.

'It's rather disconcerting to realise that while I have to ask you the simplest things about your likes and dislikes you know everything about mine,' murmured Benedict, watching her sip her coffee.

'Hardly everything,' Vanessa contested automatically.

'Still, I feel at a disadvantage.'

As a victory it was a vitally unimportant one but the knowledge that he might feel in any way insecure was a pleasing one. She couldn't help a slightly smug smile as she said lightly, 'Well, now you know how I take my coffee.'

He regarded the infinitesimal lowering of her guard blandly. 'Mmm... You may as well have something to eat, too, even though I know you're not hungry.'

Since she had been practically drooling over the array of food he had spread before her she didn't bother to protest as he cut the bacon-and-egg pie with a chased-silver knife and transferred wedges on to two plates. With a little flourish he snapped out a napkin and leaned over to drape it across her thighs before handing her the plate. 'Do you think I'd make a good butler?' he asked, tongue-in-cheek.

She was startled into uttering the truth. 'God, no!'

'That was very emphatic.' He stretched out on his side, propped up on one arm, munching at his portion of pie. 'Why?'

'Because you're not... you're too——' She stopped, wondering how much her opinion of his character was going to be given away.

'Not what? Too what?'

'Too old.'

He stopped chewing.

'The hell I am!'

Not liking the gleam in his eye that accompanied the growl, Vanessa hastened to clarify. 'Too old to change, I mean. You're used to having everything your own way. I can't see you taking orders without arguing——'

'Are we talking about you or me here?' he interrupted sarcastically. 'I'm an architect; I take orders from my clients every day——'

'I rather got the impression that you only took the orders that you *wanted* to take,' said Vanessa drily. 'Isn't that why you left your father's firm? Face it, you just couldn't cut it in a job that requires you to be constantly deferential. You have to run things, to be in charge. You wouldn't even know where your forelock was, let alone how to tug it!'

'I haven't noticed you being particularly deferential. And since when have I asked for any forelock-tugging from my employees?'

He seemed genuinely pained and she was quick to point out tartly, 'You give me time off and then expect me to be meekly at your beck and call!'

He gave her a grim smile. 'Meekly, no—I'm not that much of an optimist. But if you really didn't want to be here with me now, Vanessa, you would have driven off and left me in a cloud of dust. But you didn't. And don't tell me that it was mere deference to my authority. Your thumb your nose at *that* when it suits you. When we get down to the nitty gritty, this is between Benedict and Vanessa, man and woman, not employer and employee.'

Vanessa gave him a haughty look. 'I really don't want——'

'Yes, you do. You want me and you're afraid of it. You're afraid it makes you vulnerable. Well, hell, men are vulnerable too. Much more so. We can't hide the fact that we find a woman exciting. Look at me, do you think I *like* having such little self-control . . . ?'

He indicated his body with an impatient sweep of his hand from shoulder to hip. Not understanding his reference, Vanessa followed the gesture to its obvious conclusion and felt herself flushing at the sight of his blatant masculinity, her eyes jerking back to his sardonic expression.

'Embarrassed? Think of how I feel!'

She did and her blush deepened. He gave a barking laugh. 'Yes, well, I admit it's not *all* bad. In fact . . .' his drawl took on a husky note '. . . some of it is pretty damned good. The question is, what are we going to do about it?'

'We're not going to do anything,' said Vanessa shakily, scrabbling for her battered defences. 'And if you think that you can use sexual harassment to——'

'Sexual harassment!' He jack-knifed to a sitting position, cursing fiercely as coffee spilled across his thigh. He wiped the stain carelessly with the sleeve of his sweater as he continued harshly, 'What in the hell are you talking about?'

'About you using your. . .your position to. . .to threaten me——'

'Any threats are in your own mixed-up little mind.' She realised that this time he was genuinely angry and becoming more so with every word he uttered. 'Why should the fact that you work for me have any bearing on the fact that we find each other attractive? So I went off my head a little at first—I think I was entitled, don't you? Did I ever say I'd fire you if you don't have sex with me?'

'No, but——'

'No. I said precisely the opposite, didn't I? And have I touched you sexually against your will?'

He had hardly touched her at all in the past two weeks; that was what had made her so acutely aware of him...the fact that he was making such an obvious effort *not* to touch her. The fact that she had found herself looking at his hands and his mouth and remembering, wondering...

'No, but——'

'Have I made suggestive comments to you while we've been working on that damned book? Have I been anything but casual and friendly?'

'No, but——'

'But what? I've been walking on damned eggshells around you so as not to frighten you off, to give you a chance to get to know me as a whole person, and now you accuse me of *sexual harassment*? My God, do you really think I'm that bloody desperate? That despicable?'

He was shouting. Cool, contained Benedict Savage was shouting at her. And swearing like an explosive teenager.

'No, of course not,' she admitted weakly.

'Then would you mind telling me what *exactly* it is that I do that makes you feel so quiveringly helpless before my slavering lust?' He raked a look down her body that made her feel hot all over.

'It's that!' she blurted out desperately. 'The way you look at me.'

There was a shivering silence. Then, '*Look*? So even looking's forbidden now? I think you'll have to be a bit more precise, Vanessa.'

'I don't want to talk about it——'

'Neither do I!'

Suddenly he was no longer sitting on the other side of the blanket. With a lithe movement he lunged across the clutter between them, upsetting plates and scattering food as he came down over her, straddling her body on his braced arms and knees as she collapsed backwards in shock. 'I'd much rather *do* something about it!'

'Stop it!' she panted, pushing both hands against his chest, holding him at bay.

'Who am I?'

She blinked at him, startled, the nimbus of light around his head making it difficult for her to see his expression. 'What?'

'My name—who am I?' he demanded, allowing her the illusion of being able to keep him at arm's length as he hovered over her. 'You don't call me sir any more and you can't quite bring yourself to say Mr Savage either. But you refuse to call me Benedict. I don't like being a nobody. So why don't you try Ben? You called me that once before, remember? Short, sweet and intimate. Try it. Say Ben, Vanessa.'

'For goodness' sake——'

'Say it.' He took off his glasses and threw them away in a gesture of reckless intent that made her heart pound.

'All right, damn it—Ben!' she retorted wildly. 'There, I've said it. Ben, Ben, Ben——'

Her provocative chant was suddenly smothered. There was no tentativeness, none of the explorative gentleness that had characterised his last kiss. This time he was all aggressive, dominating male. The kiss was hot and hard, swallowing her anger and feeding it back to her piece by defiant piece. In the first few savage moments of contact he didn't even allow her the luxury of a response—biting, licking and sucking at her mouth as if he were a starving man driven to extract every scrap of nourishment from the sensual feast before it could be snatched away from him.

But even as her mouth parted helplessly under the greedy onslaught Vanessa knew that she wasn't going to deny him anything. Only Benedict could make her feel like this, so furious, so frustrated, so wildly aroused that she no longer cared about the rules and petty restrictions that she had carefully worked out to build and govern her peaceful life.

'Say it again,' his husky voice growled into her moist depths. His tongue caressed hers, stroking his name along her trembling taste-buds, teasing it out of her in an aching sigh of pleasure.

'Ben...'

He gave a low grunt of triumph and the kiss changed, hardening even further as he came heavily down on her, his lithe body crushing her into the cushioning grasses with a powerful surging movement that dislodged her feverish grip on his sweater. Her hands slid up over his shoulders and curved down over his straining back as he settled his full length intimately against her, pushing insistently at her knees until he had nudged them far enough apart to insinuate himself between them.

'God, I love the way you say my name...' He cupped her head in one hand, pulling at her scarf with the other until her hair fluffed out across the blanket, and then he nuzzled at it before returning to her mouth, this time paying thorough attention to her every response.

As his tongue licked at her senses his free hand smoothed down the side of her soft cardigan and over her denim flank to hook behind her knee, bending it up to rest alongside his hip, increasing the intimacy of the undulating pressure between her thighs in a way that made her moan.

'Am I hurting you?' he whispered harshly, lifting his mouth from hers to study her dazed expression.

'Yes...' Her eyes were closed, her face stiff with an agony of bliss that he couldn't fail to misread.

'Then let me help you, heal you...' He shifted his torso sideways and her eyes fluttered open as she felt a pearlised button between her breasts suddenly give way.

'Why is it you always wear clothes with so many damned tiny buttons?' he growled, so intent on his task that he didn't notice her watching him through wondering eyes. His face was flushed, the tip of his tongue tracing his swollen lower lip as he concentrated.

She looked down at what he was doing, shocked to discover that he wasn't bothering to undo the buttons in a proper sequence but was merely exposing her breasts as quickly as he could. Somehow it seemed more indecent that way. Instinctively she put a hand to the top button only to have it impatiently brushed away.

'No. I want to do it. I want to see.' He looked up then and his eyes were hot and dark and at least as indecent as her thoughts. He deliberately held her gaze as he undid another button and then paused, splaying his hands possessively over the twin swells of soft angora and contracting them just enough to make her gasp.

'Someone might come,' she whispered threadily, arching helplessly as his hands contracted again.

'No one can see us here. We're safely tucked up in our little nest,' he murmured, not taking his eyes off her vulnerable face as he undid the rest of the buttons by touch and slowly began to draw the loose edges of her cardigan aside, stroking the downy wool across her sensitive skin. 'You want me to look at you, don't you, Nessa, to stop this ache we both have...?'

She stopped breathing, wondering whether he would be disappointed when he finally saw the plain white bra she was wearing, serviceable rather than seductive.

He looked down and stilled, a tiny smile sizzling at the corner of his mouth at the sight of the smooth, seamless cups and the intriguing shadowy outline of her areolae traced against the silky fine fabric. 'Where does it fasten?'

It was her willingness he was requesting, not operating instructions, Vanessa realised and she responded breathlessly. 'H-here.' She pulled her arms from his neck to touch herself nervously between her breasts, her voice nearly as thick as his.

'No.' He stopped her tentative movement, catching first one wrist and then the other and pressing them down against the rug on either side of her head. She lay

quiescent as his fingers trailed slowly away to deftly
unclip the tiny catch and delicately ease her breasts free
from their aching confinement. His eyes blazed like blue
fire.

'Oh, yes...oh, darling, just look at you...' He leaned
forward and his forefinger drifted across her bare nipple
in a whisper-light caress. She flinched and he touched
her again, and again, until she was arching into the
maddeningly light caresses, needing more than this ex-
quisite teasing.

'So soft and smooth...' he murmured, absorbed in
his erotic entrancement. 'And such beautiful, velvety
pink rosebuds...look how they darken and furl so sweet
and tight when they're plucked...' His thumb and forefinger moved skilfully, sending sharp splinters of abandoned pleasure streaking to the core of her being. He
let her experience the thrill over and over again before
he finally gathered her into his cupped palms, admiring
the frame his masculine fingers created around her
overflowing ripeness, lifting her, praising her with his
eyes and words and finally, to her unbearable delight,
his mouth.

Her fists opened and closed helplessly beside her
mindlessly tossing head as he suckled his way up the
warm, creamy slopes, seeking the peaks that he had
meticulously teased to rigid excitement, nuzzling them
hotly, licking and sucking at each swollen bud in turn,
at first with extreme delicacy and then with a ravishingly
raw hunger, working on her with his teeth and tongue
until her whole body pulsed with the same powerfully
driving rhythm that rode him between her raised legs,
stroking her with his growing hardness until she was
aware of nothing else but a terrifying pressure building
up inside her.

A wave of primitive fear increased the pressure as her
body jolted with the impact of another bunching male
thrust. He was ready for her but she wasn't ready at

all—she would never be! She couldn't see him but she could feel how big he was—much bigger than Julian had been and that meant that when he lost control the pain would also be worse and the pleasure that he had given her would be nothing in comparison. She was mad, insane to think she had wanted this...

She wasn't aware of the frightened little sounds and hectic movements she was making until he reluctantly abandoned her glistening flesh to soothe her frantic cries with his mouth.

'It's all right, darling, it's all right.'

'No, no...' She was almost sobbing as she writhed beneath his thighs, torn by the devastating conflict of desire against doubt. 'It hurts——'

'I know.' He kissed her, misunderstanding, holding her tightly and groaning as his body was racked by a long shudder. 'I'm sorry, I didn't mean for us to go so far... Here, let me at least do this for you...'

She felt his hand on her bare belly, the tug on the snap of her jeans, the metallic slide of her zip, and then the long, skilful fingers were brushing through the soft thicket between her legs, finding her secret source, touching her where she was hot and damp, sliding inside with a shocking ease that sent a piercingly erotic thrill of terror shafting to her brain. She wanted it all in that instant—the pleasure, the ramming pain, the brutal, bleeding emptiness...

'No!' She went rigid and blackness came swirling in on her, the way it had that other time when the agony had been so intense that she had momentarily passed out, but this time she fought it, determined not to give in, not to be completely helpless. The darkness swirled hot and suffocating, clinging around her eyes and nose and mouth until suddenly it dissolved with an icy shock.

Her eyes flew wide and she found herself staring up at Benedict, who was kneeling over her on the rug, bathing her face and neck with a napkin dripping with champagne.

'What a dreadful waste,' she croaked automatically as she saw him clumsily slop another splash of vintage bubbly into the napkin and she gasped as he applied its wet chill to her throat.

'It's not going to be wasted, believe me.' He lifted the napkin and shocked her by applying his mouth to her foaming skin, lapping it dry with delicate, rasping strokes of his tongue. 'There. Happy? Now tell me who the hell Julian is!'

'Julian...?' The colour that had leached from her face flooded back.

'The man you seem to have got me mixed up with just now. The bastard whom you begged not to hurt you.'

She tried to struggle upright, pulling her cardigan over her bare breasts. 'I'm sorry——'

He pushed her flat again with an implacable hand. 'So am I. I want to know what he did to you. Did he rape you?'

'I...n-no.'

His mouth thinned at her uncertainty, his blue eyes glowing with ruthless intent. 'We're not leaving here until you tell me, Vanessa. I'm not going to be made to pay for someone else's crimes. Who is bloody Julian?'

She held his gaze, just. 'A man I used to know. In England.'

'Were you in love with him?'

Her eyes fluttered away from his. 'No! Yes—I don't know——'

'This isn't multiple choice. Which was it?'

He was angry, but she had the sense to know that it wasn't with her. She looked back at him pleadingly. 'Please, let me do up my cardigan first...'

For an awful moment she thought he was going to refuse, his eyes growing hungry again as they roved over her flushed, well-loved breasts, but then he muttered something violent under his breath and swivelled to rake through the debris of the picnic and find his glasses. He put them on and watched broodingly as she fumbled first with the fastenings of her bra and jeans and then started on the tiny buttons of her cardigan. When it was evident that her shaking fingers were tackling a task that was temporarily beyond their capability he took over with an impatient growl, making her painfully aware that her nipples were still stiff and throbbing from his mouth. When he had finished he caught her chin in his hand.

'Now, Vanessa. Talk.'

He was brooking no refusal and after the devastating intimacy they had just shared her resistance was wretchedly weak.

'Julian was the son of the man I was butler for in London,' she said wearily. 'He liked a challenge and I was naïve and stupid enough to present him with one. It was my first really independent job and I had no family or friends in London and the whole situation was pretty nerve-racking—Egon St Clair and his wife were going through a fairly spectacular marriage break-up and their two grown-up daughters and Julian used to turn up at the house every now and then and contribute to the shouting matches.'

She pulled herself out of his grasp and sat back, trying not to notice that Benedict's casual elegance was now sexily rumpled, the coffee-stained fabric of his trousers stretched tautly across his thighs, the sleeves of his sweater pushed up to reveal the dark hair on his arms and the steel watch glinting on his strong wrist. 'So when Julian suddenly started plying me with attention I was grateful for his kindness, and flattered . . . he was thirty, rich, handsome and sophisticated—what insignificant nineteen-year-old *wouldn't* have been impressed? And he presented this image of himself, you see, as a tortured romantic, a misunderstood poor little rich boy who secretly longed to have his rakish life redeemed by the love of a good, plain woman. Like an idiot I fell for it. But all he wanted was a one night stand, a chance to flex his ego...' All her wretched humiliation was in her voice and in the bitter smile that bracketed her wide mouth as she looked unflinchingly at Benedict. 'So you see, it wasn't rape because I went with him willingly.'

'But you changed your mind somewhere along the line, didn't you?' he said shrewdly. 'Vanessa, if he forced you at *any* point, it was rape.'

Her mouth twisted in a painful attempt to be honest. 'I told you, I *wanted* to... I *tried* to enjoy it but he—I just couldn't seem to——' She broke off and shrugged miserably, looking out to the white-capped sea. 'I don't wonder he got furious in the end.'

'Did he hit you?' he asked in a peculiarly clipped monotone.

'Oh, no, nothing like that. He was very strong; he just held me down while he—he——' She shuddered, her eyes hauntingly dark. 'I—I was badly bruised, that's all,' she ended up lamely, cringing away from the memory of the clinical details. 'And I was sick for a couple of days...' To recover just in time for the fresh storm to break over her unsuspecting head.

Benedict was too acute an interpreter of the language to miss the glaring subtext. 'He was your first, wasn't he?' he said ferociously. 'Your first lover and the selfish bastard botched it!'

Vanessa was disturbed by his relentless intensity. 'It happened years ago. It really has nothing to do with you——'

'It does if you're going to faint with fear every time you approach a climax in my arms.'

'*Benedict*!' She folded her arms protectively across her breasts as they surged back to aching life. Tiny cramps of treacherous pleasure ripped through her body, causing an immediate panic. 'I can't let it happen again,' she said desperately. 'I can't afford to get involved with you——'

'Why? I'm free, I won't cost you anything.'

His attempted lightness caught her on the raw, lancing another festering boil. 'That's what *he* said, and in the end it cost me everything I had!'

'What are you talking about?'

It was time he knew. Perhaps then this awful agony of indecision and apprehension would be over. He would reject her finally and completely before it was too late. He would fire her and she could crawl away with her pride in tatters but her fragile heart still intact.

'I'm talking about why I left England when I did,' she said in a hard voice that matched the shellac shine in her eyes.

'I had to. You see it wasn't just Julian I slept with. Oh, no. I had sex with his father, too, even though he was fat and ugly and old enough to be my grandfather. I didn't care because I knew he was rich.' The words began to pour from her in a brittle avalanche, gathering an icy momentum of their own. 'I had it all perfectly planned, you see. I insinuated myself into Egon's household and then I seduced him in the marital bed and persuaded him to kick his wife out into the street. I made sure he alienated the rest of his family and then I convinced him to write a new will that disinherited them all and left his entire fortune to me. Then he conveniently died of a heart-attack, probably because I injected an air bubble into his veins one night when we were having sex. Only the autopsy never proved it, so I got away scot-free.'

'What in the *hell* are you talking about?'

Behind the mask of his bewildered shock she knew what was happening. His fastidious mind was already beginning to recoil from the muck-racking lies. Mud sticks. That was what the St Clairs had relied on when they had started their sordid rumour campaign—Julian

included. He had robbed her almost simultaneously of
her virginity *and* her virtue. By the time the furore had
died down she had been a social and professional pariah,
clean only in the eyes of her father and Judge Seaton,
who had been a personal friend of Egon St Clair and
knew the greed and viciousness of which Belinda St Clair
and her offspring were capable. The judge had been as
shocked and angry as Vanessa that Egon had chosen to
make her an unwitting accomplice to his posthumous
revenge on his estranged wife by naming her as his heir,
thereby setting her up as the sole target of her furious
malice. He had suggested that she sue the St Clairs for
slander and the papers for libel, but Vanessa had just
wanted to put the whole horrible nightmare behind her.
She couldn't face more prying publicity; the snickers and
the pointing and the leering curiosity had sickened and
sapped her spirit almost to the point of breaking.

'Oh, don't worry. I didn't prosper from all my sordid
crimes,' she flung at Benedict in wretched defiance,
hating him for sitting there so silent, so still,
unquestioning, accepting. 'The fortune turned out to be
wildly inflated and I had to sign away my claim to avoid
financial litigation. I'm surprised you don't recall the
juicy details; it made the tabloids all over the world. It
was a story with everything—kinky sex, blackmail, fraud
and murder. You should ask to see my scrapbook some
time! Nothing ever came to court, of course, but that's
only because I was too clever for the cops—the police
couldn't dig up enough solid evidence to bring charges.
But this is probably no surpirse to you, right?' she
goaded, at the end of her tether. 'You always thought
there was something suspicious about me and the judge.
Maybe you were right. A woman with my background——'

She broke off. His head was bent, his shoulders were
shaking. He was erupting with rage, with outrage; he
was going to slice her heart out of her chest with a few

brutal words and sling her into an exile far worse than the oblivion she had already endured. But then he threw his head back and she saw that he was laughing— *laughing* ...

For a moment she thought she was going to vomit with the pain. She leapt to her feet, black dots dancing nauseatingly in front of her stinging eyes. 'Oh, so you think it's funny, do you?' she choked. 'My life being ruined is just a big joke to you——'

She whirled to run but he was up, catching her by the elbow, still laughing. 'No, Vanessa! Listen——'

'*Listen*? You——' She tried to hit him and he twisted her arm behind her back.

'I wasn't laughing——'

The blatant untruth made her twist violently. 'Let me go, you filthy liar——'

'Vanessa.' He shook her panting form roughly. 'You can't fling things like that at me in a temper and expect me to take them seriously. Besides, if that farrago of ridiculous nonsense bears any relation to reality I'll eat my hat. Of course I laughed. To anyone who knows you at all the idea of you being an evil, gold-digging vamp is totally risible. What you know about seduction can be written on the head of a pin! You have no idea what turns a man on. Now, why don't you just calm down and tell me about your deep, dark, dreaded past properly, instead of waving it in front of my face like a red rag to a bull? You got exactly the reaction you damned well deserved ...'

And so had he, thought Vanessa savagely a few fraught moments later, looking in her rear-view mirror to see the masculine figure standing in a cloud of sandy dust as she accelerated recklessly away from the beach. Was he shaking his fist at her? He was certainly furious, his last frustrated yell ringing in her ears.

'You can't run away from your emotions forever, Vanessa. I won't let you use Whitefield as your private

bolt-hole to avoid life's nasty human compli-
cations——'

At least she had got the final word in. As she'd
slammed the car door, almost catching his fingers in the
process, she had yelled back, 'Why not? *You* are! I never
believed you decided to come down to Whitefield out
of the blue just for an innocent holiday. You said you
needed to get away and Auckland was too accessible.
You're running away from something, too, so don't
preach your self-serving sermons at *me*!'

CHAPTER NINE

IT WAS a miracle that Vanessa didn't kill herself on the drive back to Whitefield. She could hardly see the road for tears and she was shaking so badly that the gears ground fiercely with every change.

She wasn't a masochist, she told herself fiercely. She wasn't going to set herself up for another lesson in the miseries of unrequited love. Back there on the beach she had realised, to her horror, that she was even more vulnerable to her emotions now than she had been five years ago. Julian's charm had been largely superficial, his character incapable of a great depth of emotion, and at some instinctual level she must have realised that, for, although his rejection and betrayal had been wretchedly painful at the time, she had survived it by despising him and forgiving herself for her immaturity.

Benedict—clever, cultured, cloaked in layers of intriguing emotional complexity—was impossible to despise. Such a serious man would never love easily—or feign love where it didn't exist—and he was cruelly honest about his intentions. He was looking for a lover, not a lifelong companion. He was rejecting her love before it was even offered.

Well, this time she was going to be the one doing the rejecting, Vanessa told herself as she spun the car recklessly into the gates at Whitefield. A volatile cocktail of temptation and challenge had temporarily deranged the molecules of her brain, that was all. Her feelings towards Benedict were pure chemistry—and she was a stout opponent of chemical dependencies.

She wasn't in love with him. She *refused* to be. She
would stick to her original plan and fall in love with
Richard and he would be kind and tender and never
terrify her with feelings she couldn't control, or force
himself into every crack and corner of her consciousness
until she felt her life wasn't her own any more!

Suddenly Vanessa slammed on the brakes, fish-tailing
the car on the gravel as she almost rear-ended the snazzy
yellow left-hand-drive Corvette parked crookedly with
its boot open on the forecourt.

A short, stocky man with rusty brown hair ran down
the steps from the house to jerk open her door so suddenly that Vanessa almost fell out at his feet.

'My God—is that you, Flynn?' he said, his incredulity
turning to frank amusement. 'I thought it was Mario
Andretti!'

Vanessa recovered herself and straightened to her full
height. 'B—Mr Savage didn't say that you were expected,
Mr Judson.'

He grinned at her stiffness, his twinkling brown eyes
curious as she tried to smooth back the curly, wind-swept
mass of her hair.

'I live to surprise him,' he murmured, pretending not
to notice the tear-stains on her cheeks. 'Though I get the
feeling that this time I'm the one in for the surprise. Mrs
Riley said you two were on a picnic. Didn't Ben come
back with you?'

'I didn't ask,' she snapped with perfect truth and
flushed as his curiosity intensified. She was searching
for some innocuous comment to temper her rudeness
when a woman emerged from the house behind him.

She was in her late twenties, petite and perfect, a
dainty, slender woman who looked as fragile as she was
beautiful, her flame-red hair emphasising the pale
translucence of her skin and the brilliance of the slanted
green eyes. Her classic suit matched her eyes and
screamed Chanel.

'Have you found out where Benedict is yet, Dane? Goodness, who on earth is this?' The amused drawl and the slow, critical sweep of the green eyes made Vanessa's hackles rise instantly.

'I'm Mr Savage's butler,' she said crisply.

'You're kidding? She's kidding, right?' The woman arched incredulous brows at Dane who shook his head with a grin as he lifted a suitcase out of his car.

Vanessa found herself on the receiving end of a careless shrug of dismissal. 'Oh, well, I suppose Benedict likes to have his little eccentricities. What does he call you?'

Darling, Vanessa was tempted to reply caustically.

'Flynn.'

'Well, Flynn, if you *are* a butler you'd better help Dane bring in the suitcases.'

'You're *staying*?' Vanessa blurted inadvertently.

'Of course we're staying,' the woman answered impatiently. From her accent she was an American and Vanessa wondered if she and Dane were an item. It was fortunate that Vanessa had assumed her professional mask of polite rigidity because the next comment came as a searing bolt out of the blue.

'I certainly didn't come all this way to be fobbed off on any hotel. Benedict and I have a lot of planning to do. He's under a lot of pressure and I can understand him needing a break, but he has to make some decision about our engagement——'

'Engagement?' Vanessa echoed helplessly.

'Yes. I'm Lacey Taylor.' She said her name as if she expected thunderous applause, or at least a glimmer of recognition. She got neither.

'He—Mr Savage never mentioned a fiancée,' Vanessa managed to say.

'Benedict is a very private man. I don't suppose he sees any need to discuss his personal relationships with domestic staff,' she was informed pointedly. 'Now, perhaps you'll direct me to my room so that I can freshen up before he gets back from wherever he's disappeared to. Come, Dane.'

Then she was gliding away, her high heels crunching prettily over the gravel.

Vanessa looked at Dane Judson blankly.

'Why do I feel like a dog being called to heel?' he said ruefully. 'If you see Ben before I do, tell him not to blame me. When Lacey gets an idea in her head it's pretty tough to shift and I didn't think Ben would appreciate her turning up here on her own.'

'But...who is she?' Vanessa was trying to come to terms with the knowledge that all the while that Benedict had been stubbornly burrowing his way into her heart he had already been committed to another woman. So much for not being able to despise him. He was *worse* than despicable!

'An architect—a very clever one, too. She works for his father's firm. Her parents are great friends of the Savages.'

Oh, great. Loaded with brains as well as beauty, and almost part of the family already. If Vanessa hadn't been so furious she would have burst into tears.

'How long have she and B—Mr Savage been engaged?'

'Ask me that again in a couple of hours and I might be able to give you an answer,' Dane said drily, picking up the two heaviest cases and carrying them up the steps, leaving Vanessa to trail behind with the other one as she turned his cryptic words over in her head.

Did he mean that the engagement had been secret, even from Benedict's best friend? Come to think of it, she hadn't noticed any engagement ring on those slender fingers...

She found out why a couple of hours later as she served afternoon tea in the drawing-room.

Whatever Benedict's relationship with Lacey Taylor, he wasn't in love with her. His body language spoke volumes. While Lacey leaned into his every word, smiled at him and laid her hand on his arm every chance she got, Benedict was all but rolled into a defensive ball of armoured politeness. Yet Lacey behaved as if his cool reserve were a gushing welcome. She didn't so much flirt as brazenly assume, and Vanessa found herself almost admiring her for her gall.

Dane, sprawling sideways in his chair, winked at Vanessa as she bent to offer him a slice of Kate's Madeira cake.

'Lucky I'm here to act as chaperon. As you can see, loverboy can hardly keep his hands off her,' he whispered wickedly.

Since Benedict had moved to stand against the window on the far side of the room to Lacey, his hands clasped firmly behind his back, the comment made Vanessa bite her lip to hold back an unprofessional smirk.

As she straightened she caught Benedict's smouldering gaze and hastily returned her mouth to its former primness.

She didn't know how he had got back to the house from the beach but it had taken him an hour and he had arrived in a full-blooded fury, slamming the front door so that the whole house had seemed to shudder and yelling for her in a voice that had promised savage retribution. Fortunately, his unexpected guests had promptly appeared to thwart his temper and since then Vanessa had been grateful to Lacey for sticking to him like fly-paper.

Now he beckoned her with an ominously grim expression, and, holding the plate in front of her like a shield, Vanessa approached him warily.

'What was he saying to you?' he demanded in an undertone as Lacey replied to some remark of Dane's. 'Whatever it was, don't believe him. I had no idea they were going to turn up.'

She looked at him serenely. 'I don't imagine you did. It must be very awkward to have your intended mistress and future wife under the same roof.'

Her cool whisper made his eyes narrow but she immediately turned away to pour the tea before withdrawing, nervously aware of Benedict's brooding gaze following every step of her dignified escape.

Later, when she was clearing away the tray, he managed to extricate himself long enough from his guests to waylay her outside the door. 'It's not what it looks like, Vanessa. Lacey's not my fiancée, damn it!' he said fiercely.

'That's odd. She seems to think she is!'

'We went out together a few times. All right, more than a few,' he admitted raggedly as she stiffened. 'But that's all we did. Go out. It was a mistake. I never asked her to marry me. You have nothing to be jealous of——'

'Jealous?' she said with coolly calculated surprise, as if the idea had never even occurred to her, and watched his eyebrows twitch sharply together into a scowl.

'Benedict——?'

He jerked, cursing under his breath at the snip of heels that accompanied the plaintive call.

'You'd better run along, Benedict,' Vanessa goaded, enjoying his harassed expression. 'Your fiancée's getting anxious.'

Dinner was even more enlightening. When Vanessa ventured into the room with the soup tureen Benedict turned to Lacey in an excellent imitation of a man to whom servants were wholly invisible and stated deliberately that, as he had already told her a number of times, he had no intention of pandering to their parents' archaic notion of a dynastic marriage between their offspring.

Her answer was to pat him condescendingly on the hand.

'Now, Benedict, aren't you carrying this rebellion against your father too far? So what if he told you he would like to see us married? That's no reason to sacrifice our future. And it's rather insulting to both of us to suggest that the only reason I could want to marry you is to consolidate our inheritances. Why, I've always adored being in your company and we get on splendidly. I don't think we've ever had an argument in all the years we've known each other! And you can't deny that our backgrounds and careers are incredibly compatible. Don't you agree, Dane?'

'Oh, incredibly compatible,' murmured Dane obediently, earning himself a ferocious look from his friend.

And so it went on throughout the entire four-course meal, Benedict baffled at every turn by Lacey's unshakeably confident belief in their shared destiny.

Seated between two men in elegant dark suits and looking quite stunning in a simple green cocktail dress, Lacey was obviously in her social element but, by the time she brought coffee, Vanessa no longer wanted to scratch out the gorgeous green eyes. She actually felt sorry for the beautiful and bossy Miss Taylor. Benedict had done everything but yawn in her face to demonstrate his lack of interest and she hadn't even noticed.

No wonder she and Benedict never argued. Lacey had obviously never roused the man behind the smooth manners and seamless sophistication.

It was evidently only with Vanessa that he was a savage, for, when she had served the final liqueurs and requested permission to retire, Benedict leaned back in his chair and asked silkily, 'Are you sleeping in your own bed tonight, Vanessa?'

The atmosphere in the dining-room dropped ten degrees in two seconds.

'I thought her name was Flynn?' said Lacey sharply.

'Flynn is her surname,' supplied Benedict smoothly, not taking his eyes off his quarry. 'Vanessa?'

She could just imagine what was going through the other woman's head. And Dane Judson's. If his eyebrows rose any higher they would disappear into his hairline.

'Yes,' she bit off, and then breached one of the cardinal rules of etiquette by delivering a gratuitous little speech about how she *used* to air the empty bedrooms.

'May I go now, sir?' she said woodenly, when this small exercise in embarrassment was over.

To her horror Benedict rose and sauntered towards her.

'Don't be so stuffy, Vanessa; we don't have to pretend to be formal in front of my friends.' He slid his fingers under her elbow and turned her towards the door, tossing casually over his shoulder, 'Excuse us for a minute, won't you?'

Out in the hall Vanessa wrenched her arm away and stormed off to the kitchen. Kate had left after she had dished up the main course and there was no one to hide behind as Benedict followed hot on her heels.

'Get out of here! Do you know what they must be thinking?' she raged at him. 'Especially after that stupid remark about where I was sleeping. I've already had my reputation stolen once by some spoiled young buck and I don't intend to have it happen again. Go back to your fiancée!'

'Oh, no, you can't convince me you still believe that canard,' he dismissed contemptuously. 'Not after you've seen her in action.' He leapt back as she angrily turned on the tap over the kitchen sink full-blast, sending a jet of water bouncing off the dessert plates, nearly drenching the front of his pale grey silk shirt.

'For goodness' sake, Vanessa, this is not about your reputation—or mine,' he said, reaching across her to turn the tap off so firmly, she couldn't get it to budge again. 'Stop trying to frighten me with your lurid past. I don't *care* what happened back in England—except that whatever mess you got tangled up in obviously hurt you badly enough to colour your whole attitude towards love and sex. I'm sorry if I seemed to treat your *alleged* notoriety lightly, but I was angry at your lack of faith in me. Whether it was a mix-up or a set-up I know you could never have done the things you claim you were accused of. That's an example of *my* faith in *you*.'

Vanessa was in no mood to be coaxed. She turned and, finding herself trapped against the sink, lifted her chin belligerently. 'So?'

'So... that pot-shot of yours on the beach about running away wasn't entirely off-target. I did desperately need a break, but for the last few weeks Lacey's been popping up wherever I go and I thought she'd never follow me here. Lacey hates small towns. Even Sydney isn't big enough for her.'

Detecting a hint of softening in her rigid expression, he moved in closer again, using the husky, confiding tone that turned her bones to wax. 'She doesn't love me, Vanessa. My parents have egged her on to think that I'm secretly dying to be drawn back into the family fold and Lacey is ambitious; she can't bear to fail—in *anything*...'

'She can't *force* you to the altar, for goodness sake,' said Vanessa, torn between anger and unwilling sympathy. Lacey Taylor did seem to be an oppressively single-minded woman. 'All you have to do is say no...'

'I have. And she tells me I'm just gun-shy about giving up my selfish, bachelor independence——'

'She's an intelligent woman; she'll get the message eventually——'

'Yes, if I'm sufficiently brutal about it in a public enough way I'm sure I can humiliate her into never even speaking to me again, but she doesn't deserve that kind of cruelty. I'm not in love with her but before she was encouraged in this fixation we had a good platonic friendship, and as a professional she still has my greatest respect.'

He took off his glasses and blinked at the harsh flu-
orescence of the kitchen lighting, and Vanessa was sunk.
'You can understand my wanting to avoid beating her
over the head with her pride, can't you, Vanessa?' he
said softly, placing his hands on either side of her on
the bench. 'If she knew I had someone else tucked away
in my life she could blame me instead of herself for her
failure to pin me down...'

His hips had crowded her buttocks against the
stainless-steel bench and the tip of his tongue was
stroking the seam of her primly sealed mouth.

'You want to pretend that we're involved?' she
murmured distractedly.

'I don't think any pretence will be necessary,' growled
Benedict, nipping at her lower lip, his thighs grinding
lightly against her.

Vanessa shivered. 'I won't lie——'

'I know. You won't have to...' He nuzzled into the
prim white collar above her jacket to kiss the betraying
pulse-beat in the curve of her throat, his hands holding
her hips as his left knee flexed, pressing inexorably
forward against the constriction of her skirt, pulling it
taut between her thighs until he was resting his knee
against the cupboard door behind her.

'She won't believe you're serious about me...not when
you could have someone like her...'

'She'll believe.' His mouth was back on hers, this time
demanding entry, his own voice thick with sensuous ab-
straction. 'If I appear to be madly in love with you her
pride will *demand* that it be very serious——'

It was like a dousing with icy water. 'If I appear'...
He only wanted the outward trappings of love, not the
sincerity that was in her heart. A lie implied was as dam-
aging as a lie spoken, as Vanessa had good reason to
know.

Lies had destroyed her ability to trust, had infected
her relationship with Benedict from the start. Secrets and

lies. She was even starting to lie to herself now, telling herself she didn't love him. And if she weakened and became his lover, who would he use in turn to get rid of Vanessa when her love became an embarrassing inconvenience?

'No——' She pulled sharply at his hair to make him release her and when he staggered back in surprise she twisted away and darted behind the kitchen table. 'No, oh, no! I'm not playing *that* game. Lacey Taylor is *your* problem, *you* deal with it. Don't expect me to help you do your dirty work!'

Something in her expression must have warned him how close she was to full-blown hysteria, because he backed off hastily, uttering soothing noises as he retreated which poured salt into her invisible wounds. She didn't want to be soothed, she wanted to be *loved*— for herself alone, without guilt or guile. And for no other reason than that she was *worthy* of being loved.

Over the next two days, however, Vanessa found her sense of proportion returning as Lacey Taylor gave no sign that she noticed anything odd in the way that Benedict and his butler cut at each other with insulting politeness. Of course, she was so busy complaining about everything from the lack of air-conditioning to the smallness of the bathrooms that Vanessa doubted Lacey had time to notice anything but her own discomfort. She made it clear that she only tolerated Whitefield because Benedict was there, although he was spending most of the day shut in his studio with his nose buried in a sheaf of 'urgent' contracts that his colleague had handily produced.

Dane Judson was quite another kettle of fish, however, and Vanessa became resigned to the casual irreverence with which he insisted on discussing Benedict with her. Dane was a cynic about life in general and love in particular, but he made Vanessa laugh and she was not unaware that he had deliberately set himself up to be an entertaining buffer. Benedict noticed, too, which didn't improve his mood, and his retaliation was to invent some entertainment of his own.

'Celebration? What kind of celebration?' Vanessa asked remotely as she faced the animated trio in the drawing-room on the third afternoon following Lacey Taylor's arrival.

Benedict's mouth twisted at her rigid lack of expression. 'What kind do *you* think it might be, Vanessa?' he taunted cruelly.

'It's a birthday party—for this creaking old inn that Ben seems to have fallen in love with.' Dane's swift reply rescued Vanessa from her vocal paralysis. A birthday, not an engagement! 'He says it opened a hundred and twenty years ago next Saturday so he's decided to have a party to mark the occasion.'

'A costume party,' Lacey announced gleefully. 'I'm going to get mine sent from the States. I know a fantastic little place in the Village...'

'Don't go overboard, Lacey; I'm throwing a casual party, not the social event of the season,' said Benedict drily. 'This is strictly for the locals who've been involved with the inn over the years so I want the atmosphere to be very relaxed and informal. Mrs Riley has said she'll arrange the catering with a community organisation that needs the funds and members of the historical society are going to rent theatrical costumes——'

'You've spoken to someone from the historical society already?' Vanessa asked, suddenly feeling a creeping sense of paranoia. Why all this sudden sociability? She didn't think he was just pandering to Lacey's boredom with the bucolic joys of small-town living.

Blue eyes gleamed, as if he knew what she was thinking. 'Mmm. Miss Fisher, actually. Such a charming, enthusiastic old lady!'

This of the twittering spinster he had driven for *hours* to avoid on the day that he arrived! Now she *knew* he was up to something. Gone was the moody, sullen stranger of the last couple of days and in his place a man who looked dangerously back in control.

'But—next *week*?' Vanessa stuttered. 'You'll hardly have time to organise invitations, let alone extra staff——'

She might have known that he'd have all the exits covered. 'The invitations can be verbal and we won't need staff. I told you, it's going to be casual, a BYO affair where everyone can feel comfortable, like a block party—except the whole community'll be involved. Most people will be happy to pitch in and help where they can. So, you'll be here, Vanessa, but in costume like the rest of us.' He leaned back in his chair and inspected her from neat crown to sensible toe. 'And I think I have the perfect costume for you...'

Right. Perfectly dreadful, no doubt! Vanessa didn't trust that crocodile smile. Before she was sucked completely into the whirlwind of activity that Benedict's brilliant idea generated, she made sure that she obtained a suitably sedate costume from Miss Fisher and had tucked it safely away in her room well in advance.

By the time seven o'clock the following Saturday evening rolled around Vanessa felt so distracted by the milllion and one calls on her attention that she had actually half wriggled into her chosen dress before she discovered that it refused to fit.

That was because it wasn't the dress she had originally hung carefully in her wardrobe. That one was plain and decorous, as befitted an authentic Victorian lady. This one was all crimson satin flounces with black piping, with a neckline that made Vanessa's eyes widen and a waist that made them water.

The other dress was nowhere to be found and when Vanessa found a box in the bottom of her wardrobe containing a stiffened black basque she knew why.

The crisp, precise writing on the lid of the box needed no signature.

I'm sure you recognise the dress. It's from the daguerreotype of Meg on the copy of the Playbill in the judge's files. I had to guess the colour, but the dressmaker assures me that the rest of it is copied faithfully from the original—hence the need for this...

And then, as if written merely as a careless afterthought, 'Do you dare?'

As if she could be manipulated by a childish challenge! Even as a child Vanessa had never been one to accept a dare without carefully weighing the risk against the all too likely consequences.

But sometimes the choice wasn't so simple, she thought, nervously remembering that Benedict had ruled that anyone not attending the party in costume would be required to pay a public forfeit. She had a feeling any forfeit he demanded of her would be considerably more trouble than taking up his stupid challenge. Maybe he *expected* her to choose the forfeit. After the difficult week she had just had, the last thing she wanted to do was to face another fraught decision.

She almost chickened out when she saw the results of her eye-watering battle with the hooks down the front of the rigidly boned corselet. Hourglass wasn't the word. From the generous flare of her hips her waist was nipped in to breathless smallness, her pushed-up breasts almost brimming over the satin demi-cups of the bodice. Against the black satin her skin looked starkly pale, the erotic contrast even more intense when she had donned the black stockings that were supported by crimson garters at mid-thigh.

'You have no idea what turns a man on.'

She certainly did now. The thought of Benedict personally choosing this time-honoured instrument of feminine torture and male titillation made her go hot all over. Practical application apart, the undergarment was frankly indecent.

Perhaps Meg wasn't a totally innocent victim of unsolicited male aggression after all, thought Vanessa as she donned the dress which now fastened easily over her compressed flesh. Thank goodness the dressmaker had included a very unauthentic zip under the arm!

Even with the dress on Vanessa found she couldn't forget what was underneath; it was physically impossible. Every breath she took was sharply curtailed by the curved bones pressing against her abdomen and the lush over-abundance crowding the low neckline kept catching her eye when she looked down. She couldn't even see her black buttoned half-boots unless she craned her neck past the wanton obstruction, she realised with a little *frisson* of wicked amusement as she brushed her loose hair and applied her make-up with a heavier than usual hand.

She was startled by the numbers already present when she had finally psyched herself up sufficiently to emerge shyly from her room a few minutes before the party was officially due to begin. It appeared that no one intended to miss a single minute of fun, and consequently masses of people had arrived early 'to help', and then decided that the best help they could provide would be to create an atmosphere of raucous conviviality!

After she had briefly checked that the women from the local school's parents' association had everything under control in the kitchen and their husbands had the bars up and running, Vanessa allowed herself to be quickly swept up in the noisy ebb and flow of friends and acquaintances and strangers, the mutual hilarity over costumes providing just the ice-breaker that Benedict had planned.

The night was fine and summery, and it wasn't long before people began abandoning the crammed house and the garage where a small stage had been set up for the band, to spread out over torch-lit grounds. The sprawling chaos provided the perfect camouflage as far as Vanessa was concerned and for the first hour, until dusk turned to velvety darkness, she flitted in wary circles, only once stumbling across Dane pouring punch behind a potted orange tree for a giggling shepherdess. His green breeches and flowing white shirt were in studied disarray—he was Don Juan, he informed her with a wink and an amused leer at her plunging neckline.

A little while later she saw Lacey at a distance, holding glittering court as an extravagant Queen Elizabeth I under the spreading elms by the lakeside bar. Benedict was one of her courtiers, unexpectedly dressed in the starkly plain black and white garb of a Puritan, and Vanessa was maliciously pleased to see how jarringly out of place he looked beside his flamboyant, red-headed Queen.

Some time later she was watching the dancing inside the cavernous garage, waiting for Richard to return with another glass of pleasantly intoxicating punch, when a black-clad arm suddenly slid around her tiny waist, drawing her sharply back against a lean, hard body.

'Hello, Meg.'

For the briefest instant Vanessa allowed herself to lean against his welcome strength.

'Benedict.'

He didn't move and she didn't turn. This tiny moment of possession was too precious, too private to be shared...even with him.

'I'd accuse you of being elusive,' he murmured, 'but in that dress I suppose it's the last thing you could be called.'

She tossed her head, barely missing his chin. 'Whose fault is that? I didn't want to wear it!'

'But you did.' His arm tightened.

'I—didn't have any choice.'

'There are always choices, Meg. The ones we don't take are often as revealing as the ones we do. Dance with me?'

He spun her in his arms and looked down at her. Not at her breasts but at her red-painted mouth. He was kissing her with his eyes. Even though he had his glasses on she felt the full impact of that look. His hand fluffed her hair. 'Dance with me, Meg?'

'I'm waiting for Richard,' she said breathlessly, sure it was the wretched basque that must be starving her of oxygen. 'He's away getting me a drink...'

He looked over her head. 'He's talking to Lacey. Let him stay away. Besides, he's not in costume.' He looked back down at her, taking off his tall buckled hat and casting it carelessly aside, revealing the cropped darkness of his hair which so suited the austerity of his garb.

'He didn't have time—he's just come back from ten days in Melbourne. He only got back tonight. He's virtually come straight from the airport.'

'Tough!' Benedict looked triumphantly unimpressed. 'He has to surrender something of value for his transgression. You can be his forfeit to me, Meg.' He began to sway, drawing her into his arms and slowly blending into the passing flow of couples.

'I didn't think Puritans did anything as frivolous as dance,' she said shakily as she instinctively matched his languid rhythm.

'Oh, we can be seduced into the sins of the flesh like any other mortal. We just take leave to feel more guilty about them afterwards.' He had both hands at her waist now, holding the centres of their bodies lightly together as he moved, the brush of his legs in their thick black breeches catching at her satin skirts.

'I'm afraid what I know about seduction could be written on the head of a pin,' Vanessa responded haughtily.

His steps faltered, but not his gaze as his mouth crooked wryly. 'What fool phrased his compliment to you so badly? True seduction isn't about *knowing*, it's about *being*...'

His eyes gravitated inexorably to the plunging neckline of her gown. His nostrils flared, his sensual memory recognising the distinctive scent rising from the warm texture of her flesh, the scent that had lingered in his bed. 'Just be you; that's all you have to do to seduce me.'

'You mean, be Meg,' she said wistfully. In this dress she wasn't supposed to be her ordinary self, she was his erotic fantasy come to life.

'I mean be Vanessa,' he told her huskily. 'Infuriating, irresistible Vanessa. Do you know why I asked you to dance?'

She shook her head dizzily, and he answered his own question with a frank explicitness that made her breathing sharp and shallow.

'I wanted to see your lovely breasts move for me. I wanted to watch them sway and ripple like cream with every tiny, delicious motion...every breath, every sigh. I remember how hot and spicy they tasted in my mouth, how taut and swollen they felt when I cupped them in my hands... Do you think any one would notice if I bent and put my mouth just *there*...in that milky soft crevice...?'

'*I* would...!' Vanessa clutched at his forearms, her shallow gasps turning to a startled moan as her head fell back and her knees sagged. The tiny red spots in front of her eyes turned black.

'For God's sake, Vanessa, don't play the swooning Victorian maiden on me *now*!' he said with rough amusement that turned to rueful dismay as she continued to sink, her back arching limply over the span of his strong hands...

He uttered a harsh sound of dismissal as someone offered assistance, half lifting, half carrying her wilting figure off the makeshift dance-floor and through the brick archways lining the back of the garage, to one of the old stable loose-boxes, kicking the bottom of the dilapidated half-door shut behind them. Here at least they were private, if not peaceful, the open half of the door letting in a flood of yellow light along with the insistent throb of music and cacophony of voices.

'Vanessa? You're not going to actually pass out, are you?' he asked with ragged humour as he propped her against the wall, protecting her bare shoulder-blades from the rough wood by sliding his arm behind her.

She pressed a hand to her compressed stomach and shook her head muzzily as she panted, 'No... I just couldn't breathe for a moment. It's being trussed up in this dress—I can't seem to breathe and dance at the same time. Thank God women liberated themselves from their corsets years ago!'

She took several more quick, heaving breaths before she became aware of the carnal expression on Benedict's face as he slowly removed his glasses.

'It wasn't the dancing that took your breath away,' he said hoarsely. 'It was me.' And having uttered that literal truth he abruptly did what he said he had wanted to on the dance-floor. The feel of his mouth sinking voluptuously into her mounded breasts made Vanessa briefly panic again and then her eyes fluttered closed and she gave up worrying about breathing altogether.

Oh, what a lovely, lovely way to die, she thought as wave after wave of suffocatingly sensual delight clogged her heart and lungs and set her blood pulsing thick and sluggish in her veins. The faint bristle on his chin rasped erotically across her tender skin as his fist caught the bottom edge of her gown, dragging it up past her calf, her knee... holding her upright against the wall with his body as he slipped his hand further up under the crushed satin flounces to stroke the strip of satiny inner thigh laid bare between the garter and basque. Rivulets of fire flowed wherever he touched and lingered...

'Open your mouth; I need to be inside you,' he groaned, pulling his arm from her back and cupping one half-exposed breast possessively as he sought her surrendering lips hungrily.

Even through layer upon layer of satin she could feel his all-consuming need and suddenly nothing mattered but to assuage it. She ran her hands up his arms to cup his head, guiding him to the pleasure of them both, gripped by a fiercely erotic tenderness, her heavy eyelids lifting just in time to see——

Richard's mixture of pained regret and embarrassment as he turned away, gallantly trying to shield the couple inside the box from the shimmering figure at his side. He wasn't quick enough. In a split-second Lacey's beautiful face ran the gamut from curiosity to shock, disbelief and anger before she spun on her heel and stalked away in defiant disgust.

Vanessa stiffened and pushed at Benedict, whose realisation that they weren't alone had done nothing to bank his desire.

'Oh, God—Richard and Lacey,' she whispered despairingly. 'They must have seen us leave the dancing, and wondered what was wrong——'

'They had to find out some time. Now maybe Wells will stop sniffing around and find his own woman...' Benedict's crudely gloating satisfaction was like a slap in the face.

She stared at him in horror. 'This was all part of some clever plan of yours, wasn't it?' she accused wildly. 'That we be seen to sneak away and Lacey follow us—that she catch us in a flagrantly compromising position...' She realised what she must have looked like with her skirts hiked up around her waist and Benedict's hand between her thighs, and on her breast. 'Oh, God, you *planned* for this to happen...'

'The hell I did! How was I to know you were going to swoon in my arms?'

'You *used* me. You promised you wouldn't, then you *used* me!' Vanessa cried. 'How can I ever believe anything you say? Oh, God, I *hate* you!'

She lashed out with a viciously closed fist and he caught it in an iron grip, jerking it behind her as he ground out savagely, 'That's *enough*!'

He caught her other wrist and clamped it with the same hand, and then dragged a weakly struggling Vanessa out of the ramshackle back door of the garage and across the unlit rear courtyard to the French doors of the library, the only downstairs room that was shut off to the party-goers. While Vanessa panted and squirmed he searched for his keys in the narrow pocket of his breeches and unlocked the door, thrusting her inside and locking it again behind him, drawing the curtains and turning on the lamp on the desk before striding to the door to the hall to make sure that that too was firmly secured. The soundproofing that had been installed with the new wall-linings created a hushed, exotic quietness as Vanessa stood, rubbing her wrists and summoning her courage finally to demand imperiously, 'What do you think you're doing?'

'I know exactly what I'm doing.' Benedict turned, stripping off his tunic and shirt as he came towards her. 'Creating the strictest privacy in which to make love to you. No distractions, no interruptions, no possible grounds for a misunderstanding later. Perhaps I can teach you to trust the pleasure I can give you, if nothing else. At least it'll be a start. Will you take off that dress—or do you want me to do it?'

Vanessa put her trembling hands to her breasts to quiet the tumult that rioted there at the sight of his powerful chest and flat belly sheened with a light perspiration that

defined the lean wedges of curved muscle as they rose
and fell with his ragged breathing. He looked as if he
had been running, his body pumped with adrenalin, his
control so finely balanced that she could see faint tremors
as opposing bunches of muscles strained against each
other in anticipation of the next explosive burst of
movement. He was the brutal image of a man primed
for sex.

He was unbuttoning his breeches now, watching her
become aware of the violence of his arousal as he exposed himself blatantly to her shocked eyes. He bent to
pull off his boots and the narrow black breeches, his
hard flanks flexing and bunching, and then he
straightened again, completely naked. Completely vulnerable. Glistening with his need . . .

'Give me this one chance, Vanessa,' he demanded, the
angry edge of his ruthless intent blunted by the flushed
fascination with which she was still staring down at his
jutting body. 'Let me show you that when I'm with you,
as far as I'm concerned, nobody else in the world
exists . . .'

Her eyes flickered up to his. Her hands fell away from
her breasts. He reached for her . . .

The cataclysm struck.

One moment Vanessa was standing before him, fully
clothed, and the next her dress was on the floor and she
was lying on the rug beside it covered by a trembling,
groaning man in the throes of urgent passion, her long
legs wrapped around his powerful hips as the excruciating pleasure that was concentrated in the thrusting
fullness that parted and penetrated her escalated to a
series of violent convulsions.

There had been no time for fear, no time to register
anything but the glory of his manhood as he had reacted
with frenzied delight to the sight of her in the satin
basque, rolling over on to his back and seating her astride
his engorged loins so that he could enjoy the sensuous

sight of her arched above him as he roughly dealt with the row of hooks, releasing her pointed breasts to the lascivious attention of his hands and mouth as he undulated beneath her, letting her control the pace until she began straining and shuddering, unsatisfied by anything less than his complete possession.

There was no pain as he turned her on her back and mounted her in one fluid movement, stretching her with his fingers to fit him, only a ferocious relief at being able to take the full length of him, to absorb and milk him of his maleness until he jerked and stiffened and uttered hoarse, guttural cries of violent gratification as she joined his fierce upheaval.

Afterwards, while they still lay co-mingled, he gentled her out of her state of shell-shocked bliss, making her blush with his lavish praise.

'You see, at least we can speak honestly to each other with our bodies,' he murmured as he reluctantly helped her to dress, kissing her breasts in tender acknowledgement of her passionate exhaustion as he zipped her up and then pulled on his own clothes, his manner redolent with possessive satisfaction. 'What could be more honest than sustained mutual passion...?'

Vanessa looked at her sinfully dishevelled Puritan as he stretched contentedly, then strolled over to unlock the hall door. He was signalling that their lovely private idyll was over already. Her heart ached for all that she now had of him...and all that she never would. Unless she risked one final dare...

'Mutual love, perhaps?' she ventured bravely.

He stood, his hand on the door-handle, looking so utterly stunned at the suggestion that Vanessa knew instantly that she had made a bad mistake.

Before she could retrieve the betraying words Benedict staggered as the door was suddenly thrust inwards against him.

Moments later, just *how* bad Vanessa's mistake had been was being forcefully rammed home to her as they were confronted by Benedict's horrified parents, who wasted no time in pointing out the appalling implications of Benedict's allowing himself to be publicly associated with a woman of Vanessa's deeply dubious background and morals. And Benedict seemed to be tacitly agreeing with every doom-laden word!

CHAPTER TEN

IT WAS dark inside the hilltop apartment and Vanessa cursed at the lack of light as her trembling fingers dropped the doorkey and she had to grope around on the cold marble floor to find it.

Then she had trouble finding the light switch and when she finally clicked it on she had to blink in disorientation as she was confronted by the white-on-white, ultra-modern room. It took a few moments for her to remember to cross to the long narrow window on her left and wave in silhouette to the man waiting on the city street below.

The yellow Corvette took off with a throaty roar and Vanessa watched the red lights glow as he took the corner at the end of the street.

She wondered why Dane was in such an all-fired hurry to get wherever he had suddenly insisted he had to go, when he had done nothing but procrastinate, delay and dawdle all the way from Thames to Auckland. What should have taken no more than an hour and a half had taken over three. He had driven at least twenty kilometres per hour under the speed-limit, stopped for petrol and oil at two different petrol stations and pulled over twice to check his 'pinging' engine.

Then, just past Huntly, he had decided he was ravenous and had pulled into an all-night truckers' restaurant and ordered a huge meal which he had taken ages to eat, all the while plying a white-faced Vanessa with coffee and trying to persuade her to reinterpret the scene which had prompted her midnight flight from Whitefield without even so much as a change of clothes or a toothbrush. She had even had to borrow Dane's car-coat to cover the crumpled satin costume she wore in order not to create a riot among the truckers.

Somehow it had seemed symbolic that she had left Whitefield as stripped of possessions as she had been of pride. Lacey's malicious introduction of Vanessa to Benedict's parents as his lover-cum-butler couldn't have been better timed to create maximum shock and embarrassment...especially since it was obvious to them all what had been going on in the locked library.

The older couple had heard of the party from Lacey and had duly decided to make a flying visit, expecting to be able to offer their congratulations on what they assumed to be their son's engagement to a most eminently suitable young lady. Instead they had been confronted with graphic evidence that he had fallen into the clutches of an appallingly unsuitable, social-climbing hussy.

Vanessa had had to bear the shame of hearing Aaron Savage tell his son, 'For God's sake, if you want to sleep with the servants at least have the decency to be discreet about it!' and his mother frigidly suggest that whatever he was paying her it was obviously too much!

'A female butler! I always wondered what possessed you to agree to such a questionable arrangement,' Denise Savage had said in cut-glass accents of brittle disdain. 'And now my worst fears have been justified!

'Don't you care about the pain you're causing your father and I? Do you know the damage this could do to the family's reputation if it got into the papers? Goodness knows, there are certain people who would leap at the chance to use a scandal to embarrass your father. Whatever you do inevitably reflects directly on us... And you're not really being fair to this...this *person* either. Is she really someone you'd be comfortable introducing to our friends? Of course not...because it's all in such appalling bad *taste*, Benedict. Even if you're temporarily blinded by infatuation you must realise that we'd be a laughing-stock if you tried to introduce her to society...'

There had been more in that vein and Vanessa had kept waiting for an angry Benedict to leap in and defend her honour. But he had remained silent and when she'd finally tried to interrupt on her own behalf Benedict had coldly told her to be quiet and let him hear everything his parents had to say.

In the end, she had walked out in such a blind agony that she had nearly trampled Dane as he hovered by the door. Benedict had been so absorbed in what his parents were saying that he hadn't even noticed her go and, looking back over her shoulder one last time, Vanessa had numbly realised the true extent of the family resemblance.

Benedict's face had worn the same expression of pale hauteur that his mother's habitually did and his arrogant stance had been so similar to his father's that it had been almost like seeing the same man reflected through an age-distorting mirror. Perhaps his fling with her had been just one last act of rebellion against the inevitable genetic trap.

She'd been walking down the driveway towards the gates of Whitefield in a zombie-like state when Dane had caught up with her, and when no amount of desperate pleading could divert her from her obsession with getting to the airport in Auckland by whatever means she could, hitch-hiking—even walking every step of the way if she had to—he had eventually agreed to drive her. She had to go home, she'd kept repeating. She was running to the only haven left to her, the home of her heart—her family—to the love and understanding of her father in Los Angeles. *He* had never been ashamed of her...

She had fiercely refused to go back to the house even to pack, nor would promise to wait for Dane while he did so, and in the end he had given in to her fragile mental state and got his car.

While he drove he had talked incessantly, telling her what a great guy Benedict was, deep down, and how, if Vanessa was in love with him, she owed it to him to give him the benefit of the doubt; that Benedict's parents were knee-jerk reactionaries; that she shouldn't do anything rash, like leaving the country, without talking to Benedict first.

Vanessa had refused to respond until he had pointed out to her, when they were nearly to Auckland, that since she had neither money nor passport she couldn't leave the country immediately anyway. He had kindly insisted she stay at his apartment for the rest of the night, until she could call her father and 'reorientate' herself. By that time all Vanessa had wanted to do was crawl into a bed, bury her head in the pillow and have a good, long, private bawl!

She was a bit disconcerted that, after hours of relentless over-concern, Dane had casually dumped her on his doorstep with his key and a casual 'good luck', but she supposed he was respecting her desperately obvious need for privacy. Equally obviously he would have no trouble finding a bed elsewhere.

Bed...

Wearily, she turned towards the spiral staircase that Dane had included in his verbal sketch-plan and plodded upwards. She couldn't ever remember having felt this hopelessly bone-weary before. She shook her head to try and clear the miasma of exhaustion that thickened her thoughts.

The first room at the top of the stairs was a bathroom and when she clicked on the light and caught sight of herself in the mirror Vanessa shuddered. She looked even worse than she felt. The crimson dress was tawdry and garish against her bloodless skin and she could see several faint, reddened marks on her breasts from Benedict's lovemaking. Was this what his parents had seen? This...brazen doxy. No wonder they had been so horrified!

Vanessa was suddenly acutely aware that she was still perfumed with the fragrance of her abandon. She could smell Benedict on her skin. With shivering haste she shed the wretched gown and the indecent garment underneath.

The hot shower did its job, easing her aching body and cleansing away the intimate evidence of passion, although nothing could wash away the tiny, tender abrasions on her breasts and stomach and thighs. Weak tears mingled freely with the pulsing water over her face as she began to wonder what she had forfeited by her cowardice. If Benedict hadn't fought for her honour, neither had she made any attempt to fight for his. What if he, too, was alone and hurting right now...?

Pushing away the painful thought, Vanessa blotted herself on the thick white towel from the heated rail and rubbed half-heartedly at her steam-damp hair, discarding the towel listlessly on the floor with uncharacteristic untidiness before padding naked into the only other room on the mezzanine floor.

In the hint of clouded moonlight from the window she was aware of the vague, shadowy outline of a bed by the far wall but she ignored it, drawn across the room by the melancholy sight of the sleeping city. The view led in a direct line across the bricks and blocks of the central commercial district to the moon-struck waters of the Waitemata Harbour. Moon-struck. That perfectly described Vanessa. She wallowed for a moment in her splendidly miserable, self-induced isolation.

She turned on the standard lamp that she had nearly knocked over as she approached the window, and unlatched the fastening on the casement so that she could open it wide, breathing in the faintly metallic air of the city and momentarily enjoying the faint tightening of her bare skin at its cool touch. She must start to do this now, appreciate the small joys of life, since she was making such a mess of the larger ones.

She turned, a wistful smile of self-derision on her lips, and froze.

The big, wide double bed was already occupied.

The pool of light spilling across the floor from the lamp behind her was more than sufficient to reveal that the occupier was a man. He was sprawled on his stomach, his arms spread-eagled, his face buried in one of four huge pillows that were propped up in a row against the headboard.

Vanessa closed her eyes and shook her head sharply, sure that it was a fatigue-induced illusion.

She looked again, moving hesitantly towards the bed, still unwilling to trust the evidence of her tear-swollen eyes.

Above the white silk sheets, which were bunched carelessly low on his hips, the interloper's long, naked back was lean and densely muscled, faintly gleaming in the muted light, as smooth as tan-coloured satin and rippling faintly with each slow, sensuous breath. Under the arm outflung towards her she could see a thick drift of silky-soft black hair and, just above the edge of the sheet, the taut rise of the twin globes of his buttocks revealed a dusting of similar, very fine black down.

A powerful sense of bitter outrage gripped Vanessa. How *dared* he?

She began to bend and suddenly every muscle in that long, sexy, naked male back tensed and he rolled over and she found herself staring into a very wide-awake pair of grave blue eyes.

'Hello, Goldilocks. What took you so long?'

She was stunned by the warmth of desiring in that soft, whimsical growl. 'W-what are you doing—how did *you* get here?'

He shook his head back and forth against the pillow.

'Oh, ye of little faith,' he murmured, with such aching gentleness that she felt weak. Her knees swayed against the mattress and he came up on one elbow and caught her wrist, applying just enough pressure to sit her down on the edge of the bed, facing him. In her shock she forgot that she was nude and he ignored her state of innocent unawareness with gentlemanly tact.

'Where else should I be but here—with the woman I love?' he asked quietly.

It was a dream, a wishful dream.

'This is Dane's bedroom——'

'Oh, no.' His mouth curved at one corner. 'My friend has much better preservation instincts than that. This is *my* apartment, Nessa. That's where you were always going to eventually end up. In *my* bedroom, in *my* bed . . . in *my* life.'

The last was the most devastating. She trembled, brushing at her damp hair with her free hand, unaware that her bare body was revealing the welcome that she could not yet dare admit. 'But . . . you can't be here——'

He kissed the strong, slender wrist that he held, watching her intently as he drew her hand down to his chest and she couldn't help noticing that he had a number of reddened marks which were the feminine version of the brands she wore. He held her hand against his strongly arhythmic heartbeat. 'Does this feel like an illusion?

'Dane called me on his cell-phone from the first garage he called at. I made him promise to bring you here but to delay long enough to let me get here first. Thank God the pilot who flew your dress down is a teetotaller, because I'd invited him to the party and I just grabbed him and made him an offer he couldn't refuse. I wouldn't even let him stop to change on the way to the airport. It's the first time I've ever flown anywhere with a giant bat at the controls.'

Vanessa almost giggled in spite of herself. Then she remembered, and her face acquired a painful stiffness.

'W-what did your parents say?'

He sat up, the sheet dipping dangerously in his lap, his faint smile fading as he said, choosing his words carefully, 'They're my parents, Vanessa. I may not like them very much sometimes but they'll always be my parents. If you're going to be a permanent part of my life then they'll be a permanent part of yours, and we'll have to learn to deal with them together. But last night I had to let them run out of steam before I had any hope of getting them to listen. I know from bitter experience that trying to argue with them point by point only lets *them* control the confrontation. So they stated their ignorant misconceptions, and afterwards I set them straight. I told them that I loved you. That if it came to forcing me to choose between them and you, you would *always* win. They probably won't speak to us for a couple of years after we're married—in fact, if we're lucky, for *more* than a couple of years—but I'm their only son and I doubt if they'll risk cutting the ties completely...'

Vanessa's eyes were dark with anguished desire. He was talking about permanency...about loving *her*. About *marriage* ... as if they both knew they were foregone conclusions. 'The things they said—— When you told me to be quiet, let me go like that, I thought——'

'I told Lacey to leave, too,' he interrupted flatly. 'There were some things that I needed to say to them in private—old scores to settle, you might say, and some groundrules to lay for the future. They won't ever speak to you or of you like that again.' He sighed. 'I suppose I should have realised that any mention of the fatal word "scandal" was bound to spook you badly. My only excuse is that at the time I was so euphoric that you had trusted me enough to mention love that it never occurred to me that you would suffer another crisis of faith so soon afterwards...'

'I—you just looked so shocked when I said it——'

'I was. I couldn't believe it was so easy. I knew I could make you feel passion, and I was using that for all I was worth, but I didn't think that I had yet impressed you sufficiently to winkle your heart out of its tight little refuge...'

'Oh, I found you very impressive!' Vanessa teased, suddenly brimming with confidence as she ran her hand down the centre of his chest to his navel, and below to where his skin began to pale. 'Arrogant, but extremely impressive.' Her fingertips dipped under the sheet.

He sucked in his belly with a savage hiss. 'Brazen hussy,' he said thickly, reaching out to cup her breasts and massage the stiffened nipples. 'No wonder you create a scandal wherever you go. You won't have to inject me with anything lethal, darling; just keep on doing what you're doing with that hand and I'll have a little death all on my own...'

He had thrown out the metaphors deliberately, but Vanessa's radiance remained undimmed. Her certainty that she was loved gave her the security to laugh at her former fears. Her eyes gleamed with wicked, sultry knowledge as she chuckled huskily. 'Is that your idea of trying to desensitise me?'

He groaned, his hips arching off the bed, thrusting himself into her hand. 'I think it's me who needs desensitising. I meant to take it very slow with you that first time because I was afraid of hurting you, but then you were so damned responsive, I got carried away. I was afraid you might think I was no better than that bastard who hurt you...that you were disappointed...'

'It all happened so fast, I didn't have time to be disappointed,' said Vanessa, so blandly reassuring that for a moment he took her seriously and looked deeply chagrined.

Then his smile was every bit as sultry as hers as he kicked off the sheet and pulled her full-length on top of him. 'You know, Goldilocks, you haven't said you'll marry me yet; maybe I should threaten to withhold my favours until you agree.'

'If you do I'll haunt you,' Vanessa said huskily, wriggling experimentally and making them both shudder.

'Oh, yes, please...' He groaned expressively. They both laughed and he kissed her. 'We'll live at Whitefield, shall we? You running the hotel and me designing eccentric little houses. And who knows? Maybe...' He stopped suddenly and his eyes flickered. He nudged her nose with his. 'Nessa... remember how I teased you in the restaurant about being pregnant...?'

'Yes.' She knew what was coming and turned her face into his chest to smile. A few weeks ago, even an hour ago, it could have been a potential tragedy; now it was a symbol of the joy they would share in the years to come.

'I—er—when we... in the library... I know this was incredibly irresponsible... but I forgot to, you know...'

She was tempted to tease him for his unaccustomed coyness but she regarded him with tender brown eyes instead, watching an insufferable smugness settle over his beloved features as she said pertly, 'I suppose I *had* better agree to marry you, then. It wouldn't do to add illegitimacy to all the scandal I'm bringing down on the Savage family.'

'The only scandal around here, Nessa, darling, is that I love you so much I'm going to disgrace myself if you don't let me demonstrate it *right now* ...'

HARLEQUIN  PRESENTS®

Don't be late for the wedding!

Be sure to make a date for the happy event—

The first in our tantalizing new selection of stories...

Wedlocked!
Bonded in matrimony, torn by desire...

Next month, watch for:
A Bride for the Taking by Sandra Marton
Harlequin Presents #1751

Dorian had a problem, and there was only one solution: she had to become Jake Prince's wife! Jake was all too willing to make love to her, but they both knew their marriage was a sham. The trouble was, Dorian soon realized she wanted more, much more, than a few nights of bliss in his arms and a pretense of love—she wanted that pretense to become reality....

Available in July wherever Harlequin books are sold.

Take 4 bestselling love stories FREE
Plus get a FREE surprise gift!

Special Limited-time Offer

Mail to Harlequin Reader Service®

3010 Walden Avenue
P.O. Box 1867
Buffalo, N.Y. 14269-1867

YES! Please send me 4 free Harlequin Presents® novels and my free surprise gift. Then send me 6 brand-new novels every month, which I will receive months before they appear in bookstores. Bill me at the low price of $2.44 each plus 25¢ delivery and applicable sales tax, if any*. That's the complete price and a savings of over 10% off the cover prices—quite a bargain! I understand that accepting the books and gift places me under no obligation ever to buy any books. I can always return a shipment and cancel at any time. Even if I never buy another book from Harlequin, the 4 free books and the surprise gift are mine to keep forever.

106 BPA ANRH

Name	(PLEASE PRINT)	
Address	Apt. No.	
City	State	Zip

This offer is limited to one order per household and not valid to present Harlequin Presents® subscribers. *Terms and prices are subject to change without notice. Sales tax applicable in N.Y.

UPRES-295 ©1990 Harlequin Enterprises Limited

HARLEQUIN PRESENTS®

Dark secrets...

forbidden desires...

scandalous discoveries...

an enthralling six-part saga from a bright new talent!

HEARTS OF FIRE
by Miranda Lee

This exciting new family saga is set in the glamorous world of opal dealing in Australia. *HEARTS OF FIRE* unfolds over six books, revealing the passion, scandal, sin and hope that exist between two fabulously rich families. Each novel features its own gripping romance—but you'll also be hooked by the continuing story of Gemma Smith's search for the truth about her real mother, and the priceless Black Opal. And her fight for the love of ruthless seducer Nathan Whitmore...

Coming next month

Book 1: *Seduction & Sacrifice* by Miranda Lee

Everyone warned Gemma about Nathan, but she believed he wasn't heartless—just heartbroken! Clearly, he was still in love with his ex-wife, Lenore, so Gemma knew she must hide her overwhelming attraction to him....

Harlequin Presents #1754: you'll want to know what happens next!

Available in July wherever Harlequin books are sold.

HARLEQUIN®

PRESENTS Plus

Presents Plus—the power of passion!

Coming next month:

Edge of Deception by Daphne Clair
Harlequin Presents Plus #1749

Tara's ex-husband was getting married—but, five years
after their bitter parting, it finally dawned on Tara that
she still loved him! She knew it was a hopeless love.
Their past had been shadowed by an edge of deception,
and neither could forget that he'd accused Tara of an
unforgivable sin....

and

Enemy Within by Amanda Browning
Harlequin Presents Plus #1750

Ryan Douglas was simply the wrong man for Michaela!
His reputation as a womanizer was legendary, and he
was convinced Mickey had encouraged her half sister
to run off with his wealthy nephew. Now Ryan was
determined to find the missing pair—and insisted
Michaela join him!

Harlequin Presents Plus
The best has just gotten better!

Available in July wherever Harlequin books are sold.

PPLUS26

HARLEQUIN PRESENTS®

Announcing
the New Pages & Privileges™ Program
from Harlequin® and Silhouette®

Get All This FREE
With Just One Proof-of-Purchase!

- **FREE Travel Service** with the guaranteed lowest available airfares plus 5% cash back on every ticket
- **FREE Hotel Discounts** of up to 60% off at leading hotels in the U.S., Canada and Europe
- **FREE Petite Parfumerie** collection (a $50 Retail value)
- **FREE $25 Travel Voucher** to use on any ticket on any airline booked through our Travel Service
- **FREE Insider Tips Letter** full of fascinating information and hot sneak previews of upcoming books
- **FREE Mystery Gift** (if you enroll before June 15/95)

And there are more great gifts and benefits to come!
Enroll today and become Privileged!

(see insert for details)

 PROOF-OF-PURCHASE

Offer expires October 31, 1996

HP-PP2